boilerplate
C000205709

Street Life

An Anthology of Short Stories in Aid of Emmaus Cornwall.

Blue Poppy Publishing

Foreword

I do hope that you will enjoy reading this book of short stories, all revolving around the theme of homelessness.

The authors have very generously donated these stories to raise funds for Emmaus Cornwall as all the profits from the book will go to the charity.

Emmaus Cornwall is a charity that strives to open a community in Cornwall for the homeless. An Emmaus community offers people a room for as long as they need it, and work in the social enterprise that helps fund it.

If when reading you find an author who grabs your attention, their website links and/or credits are there for you to discover more of their work.

So, get yourself something to drink, put your feet up and be whisked away to another world. Enjoy!

Sue Trewella
(Chair of Emmaus Cornwall)

Acknowledgments

Thank you to everyone who has so willingly contributed a story for this anthology, without them this project would not have been possible.

To Helen Hollick and Helen Garlick for their stories and guidance, and to wonderful Oliver Tooley of Blue Poppy Publishing who has helped to educate me about the tricky world of publishing and has agreed to publish *Street Life* for Emmaus.

Thank you to Bruce Aiken not just for his story but for dealing with all the formatting, typesetting, and technical stuff for us, and to Cathy Helms for designing the evocative cover. Cathy is a professional graphic designer, who has also donated her time for free.

Above all, my deepest thanks go to my friend Liz Spear for her continuing support and encouragement. She not only suggested this idea, but also collected the stories to be printed. This book would not have existed without her.

Finally, thank you to all of you who have bought a copy of *Street Life* you are helping Emmaus achieve their goals.

CONTENTS

Trooper	Elizabeth Revill	1
An Angel Under Moonlight	Ben Fielder	10
The Homeless Poltergeist	Joe Talon	19
Dispossessed	Helen Hollick	34
Desert Boots	Bruce Aiken	40
But for the Grace of God	Ian Riddle	46
Homeless	Glenda Bartlett	58
Homeless Hope	Sarah Luddington	61
Samphire	Michael Forester	70
The Storyman	David Luddington	83
Homeless	Helen Garlick	112
The Wall	Mark Blackburn	117
Another Day	Tim Prescott	121
Tom	N. Joy	124
The Bet	Tom Barfett	129
In Chancery	Lucienne Boyce	132
Tried	Colin Leamon	144
The Veteran	Elizabeth St.John	149
Not Just Anyone	Richard Williams	154
Domino	Elizabeth Revill	161
Our Authors		177

Trooper

by Elizabeth Revill

The scruffy grey and black fluffy mongrel scooted around the corner with his tail between his legs. He dodged another stone hurled at him by a young lad who laughed viciously as the pebble skimmed the animal's back, cutting into his fur and almost slicing through his skin to his backbone. The mutt yelped and ran harder in a desperate attempt to flee the bullying thug. He dived through some shrubbery and shivered miserably behind a blackcurrant bush.

Moonshine pooled on the path behind him like spilled milk. The opalescent sheen of light became mottled as wisps of travelling night clouds attempted to mask the baleful face of the moon.

The cruel boy with the spiked gelled hair ran past whooping in glee. Trooper followed the delinquent with his eyes, eyes that had more knowledge than a dog should. His head dropped and he hardly dared to move or breathe until he felt the danger had passed.

Trooper was a free spirit. Born into a loving family the dog knew he was different. He still did all the doggy things in the same way as his canine friends so as not to alert suspicion but he possessed knowledge and understanding, which surpassed that of other creatures.

After his family moved house he had been left behind. He knew they hadn't wanted to leave him and if he hadn't gone chasing after a saucy French Poodle who had waggled her butt at him he would have been safely stowed in the family car and followed the removal truck that had taken his home, bed and all his creature comforts to their new address.

He reprimanded himself as old habits die hard, to use a cliché. How did Trooper know that? He couldn't explain it but somehow he did. It was strange, Trooper had the ability to think and reason and remember, but why?

His comfortable life was now all but a distant memory. Trooper had forgone his cosy loving home for the freedom and danger on the streets and although at first it had seemed exciting. He was now scared, tired of living on his wits and very hungry. He huddled quietly behind the bush and waited until he was sure the ruffian had moved on knowing the malevolent youth would be eager to torment some other stray or lost pet.

Trooper whimpered softly and lay down, his head on his paws, uncertain what to do or where to go next. He felt that there was a reason for his existence, a reason why he hadn't settled happily with his kind and adoptive family, a definite reason, and a reason he was destined to learn. His heart and mind told him that what would be would be. Words floated around his brain, 'everything happens for a reason.'

It was then he heard the music. He lifted his head and cocked it on one side. The lilting piano music was mournful but penetrated his soul. It awakened in him a need, a need for the warmth of loving human contact. But more than that it stirred in him a memory. Trooper knew that music and knew that delicate touch on the piano keys.

The young dog looked warily about him. The desire to search out the source of the music was strong. Should he leave the apparent safety of the bush and seek out the plaintive notes that called to him? Or should he use it as a diversion to escape the impoverished neighbourhood he had been trapped in? It was no good. Something stronger was calling him, something intangible, something inexplicable. The problem was Trooper's memories were not complete. It was if he was trying to grasp handfuls of fog to bottle and keep. There was always something missing.

Trooper hauled himself along on his tummy keeping low

and crept along the path. His belly fur became more matted and encrusted with dirt as he scrawled along the ground, skirting over mud and puddles.

He whined softly in his throat. His little heart beat erratically but still he edged forward seeking to find the delicate harmonious piano symphony, which drifted on the night air. He knew when he found the source he would find his answers. There he would learn why he was able to think and reason as he did.

The little dog had reached the outskirts of the run down estate on the edge of town. There was a busy road to cross and beyond that was the safety of trees, countryside and that music.

He still heard the music in his head although Trooper knew that was impossible. The thunderous rumble of cars and lorries flashing through the night had all but drowned out the melancholy sound. Only when there was a lull in the monotonous drone of revving engines did the tune travel on the night breeze. His acute hearing picked up the sound easily.

Trooper stopped his stealthy crawl and stood up. He shook himself to remove the excess water and soil debris from his fur and scrambled under the wooden fence marking the boundary of the slum estate. Feeling more secure and confident he slid down the green embankment coming to a stop on the edge of the asphalt highway and waited.

His eyes alert as those of an owl prowling for prey watched and he paused. Vehicles roared past. No one took any notice of the little dog sitting patiently waiting to cross.

The route to the centre of the motorway although not far in terms of distance seemed almost out of reach such was the speed of the traffic as people raced to their destinations. Trooper waited. After a lorry and drag roared by eagerly followed by a convoy of smaller vehicles there was a gap. Trooper ran to the central reservation and crouched down. His little heart was thumping so loudly it drowned out the bellowing traffic but still he could hear and feel the music in his soul.

3

Fleetingly he received an image of an attractive woman with burnished chestnut hair sitting at a piano lost in the plaintive tune she played. Her body swayed, her eyes were closed and Trooper was filled with great sadness.

Another truck rattled past disturbing his reverie. He watched the approaching cars. There were fewer vehicles running in this direction and it wasn't long before he could sprint to the other side.

His small pads skidded to a stop on the hard shoulder and he clambered up the bank. For some reason he was consumed with nervous apprehension. His stomach twisted into wringing knots and he tried to quell the seemingly irrational grip of fear.

Trooper burrowed under the chain link fence and stepped into the trees that graced the edge of the land. He was surefooted in his loping stride and he ran spurred on by something that was calling him.

A nightjar shrieked on its nocturnal hunt as it foraged for food. Trooper's ears lifted up; pricked to attention to capture and savour all he could hear. He ran on through the woods, across a stream, passing small roe deer exploring the space and nibbling the soft new shoots that sprouted from young saplings.

On and on he travelled. "It's like the Incredible Journey," thought Trooper and then stopped suddenly. What was the incredible journey? How did he know about it? Why had he thought about it? Trooper shook his coat, sat and listened, his head on one side, trying to capture the direction of the melody, which he could hear more clearly and was becoming stronger.

Other sounds filtered through into his consciousness, which spurred him to take cover. He disappeared inside a hollow tree trunk and waited. Two men crashed past through the undergrowth. Twigs cracked and snapped. He caught a fleeting glimpse of a burly, stocky man in a thick padded jacket with a rifle slung over his shoulder. His companion was a scrawny youth with acne pitted skin and patchy whiskers as if he was too young to grow a beard. They emitted a sour acrid smell. Trooper

4

almost whimpered in fear but knew he dared not make a sound. The smaller man carried a large canvas bag and the older man wore a ski mask that obliterated his broad features and he carried a brace of rabbits.

The men moved on in the direction of a country village where few lights could be seen. Most people were safely asleep in their beds but one or two properties with lights blazing indicated the occupants were awake.

Trooper crept out of hiding and followed. The men marched through the field toward the first farmhouse where they appeared to bid each other goodbye. The gangling youth took the rabbits and hurried toward a small outbuilding on the adjacent farmland. The bigger man put his masked face up to the leprous moon, which reflected in the light of man's eyes.

Trooper shuddered. He didn't like what he saw. The eyes revealed an alien presence of one that had resided with demons in hell. The man's head snapped around to the sound of the music and stepped out with renewed vigour to the isolated cottage close to the village church. The dog followed cautiously, careful to remain hidden and like a sniper on a mercenary mission held back just enough not to attract any attention.

A gravel path led to the front door of the lonely farmhouse. The man's boots crunched loudly on the small stones. He stepped off onto the soft grass to mask his approach and ventured like a fugitive toward the window where a piano played.

The poacher ducked down out of sight and peered in through the softly lit window. The drapes were open and shielded the woman's view of the night, whilst marauding intruders were able to watch at their leisure.

The man divested himself of his coat and laid it out on the grass, next to his rifle. Underneath he wore a ripped, tatty tee shirt that had faded proclaiming the slogan, 'Life or Death. You choose.'

Trooper watched.

The man continued to peer into the room. His hand drifted to his groin and he began to rub himself through his heavy denim jeans. As if that wasn't and wouldn't be enough he stopped, picked up his firearm and tiptoed around the house out of sight.

Trooper whined gently in his throat. He trotted to the window and looked in on the scene. A small growl erupted in his throat as he recognised the woman and he tried to suppress the soft mewling that threatened to burst from him. Trooper's gaze fixed on the woman. His eyes filled with unconditional love and he knew he had to get inside.

There was a splintering crunch as the thickset man burst in through the door and broke into the music room. The woman stopped playing and her hand flew up to her throat in horror as the man was upon her. He ripped her from the piano stool and flung her onto the sheepskin rug where she lay paralysed with fear.

She looked too terrified to scream although she attempted to cry out but no sound would come. The beast straddled her struggling crazily with his trouser zip. He pinned her down quite easily.

She was slim and small in stature almost ethereal looking with her cloud of chestnut tresses, dressed in a white transparent robe, which revealed her body's curvaceous silhouette.

Trooper growled more angrily now, he drew his lips back in anger revealing his wolfish teeth. His hackles rose and he knew he had to do something.

The dog ran back from the window and loped forward, taking a giant leap into the air. Without thinking the little dog hurled himself at the glass pane, which shattered with such ferocity that glass shards exploded onto the floor and rained down onto the man's back.

Trooper jumped onto the brute's shoulders and sunk his teeth into the man's neck growling like a ravaged bear. The man flailed his arms attempting to fling the animal off but Trooper clung to him like a terrier would savage a rat. He would not let go. His grip was so tight that blood began to flow from the man's neck and down his chest.

The young woman crawled away from the brutal assault and took cover under the piano. Her face was constricted with fear. She watched as the man rose up and danced in agony trying to shake off the young dog. As if coming to her senses, she emerged from hiding and grabbed the rifle firing a shot into the ceiling.

The man's eyes now filled with fear and loathing as he stumbled toward her but still Trooper held on tightly. He twisted and turned, this way and that as the young woman now woken from her stupor rushed to the phone and dialled nine, nine, nine.

Her voice was clear and resolute in spite of a slight tremor. "Police please. I'm being attacked. A man has broken into my house and has tried to rape me. My dog is keeping him at bay. The Granary… Yes… Next door to the church. Please hurry." She replaced the phone keeping the gun trained on him.

The beast managed to grasp the animal and tear him off his back. He flung Trooper at the woman and fled, leaving his rifle in her hands. The dog's teeth had slashed his throat and he was bleeding profusely. He was lucky that his artery had not been severed.

The man blundered out and made his escape. Trooper looked up into the face of the woman that he knew so well and whined softly at her. She lay down the gun and stooped to ruffle his fur. He licked her hand gently and rolled over. The woman sat down on the settee and called the mongrel to her. "You saved my life. If it hadn't been for you… " She stopped and choked back a sob, "If you don't have a home. You have one now with me."

She patted the seat next to her and Trooper jumped up and snuggled into her. Sirens could be heard approaching as a police car made its way through the village to the converted barn known as the Granary.

Trooper gazed around the familiar room, the plaster cast whorls, the splashes of aubergine that lifted the magnolia of the walls, the heavy dark beams and lovingly chosen furniture. His eyes caught the picture framed on the table of his beloved Alice in happier times with him. He jumped off the sofa and trotted to the piano and barked at the picture. She crossed to him and picked up the photograph and returned to her seat.

Trooper followed.

She smoothed down his fur and as if feeling a need, a compunction to talk, the words flooded from her.

"That's me, five years ago." Trooper barked and whined putting a paw out to try and swipe at the picture. "And that was my husband, Jake. I loved him desperately but he was killed in a road accident. So sad." She paused as she remembered, "Things were just getting back on track. We were rediscovering the joy of each other after all that pain. He'd had an affair, you see, with another teacher at school. He taught English. She taught French. He regretted it. I know he did. It was senseless, meaningless and damaging but we would have got through it. It would have made us stronger..." Alice sighed and a tear escaped her eyes as the sirens grew louder and police lights reflected around the room.

Two coppers entered and noted the disarray, broken glass and mess. Alice handed them the rifle, which one of them recognised. They exchanged a glance before sitting down and Alice began her statement. She concluded, "If Trooper here hadn't come to my aid... I shudder to think what would have happened..."

The dog looked up at the sound of his name and Alice whispered, "I'm calling you Trooper. We always said when we got a dog that's what we'd call him. I know Jake would be pleased."

The police finished taking notes and called for someone to

come and board up the window until a replacement could be fitted. One of them radioed ahead to call for a warrant to arrest Colin Beer. After checking that she would be all right they left Alice and Trooper together and drove off into the night.

Alice looked deep into Trooper's eyes. "You have an old soul," she pronounced. "I can see it... in fact you have eyes like Jake. He had those spaniel eyes that were so expressive... just like you."

Trooper licked her hand again and snuggled up to her. He was home, where he belonged and although not quite as he wanted to be. It would be enough.

An Angel Under Moonlight

by Ben Fielder

(This story contains language of a sensitive nature, but is not intended to offend.)

George turned off the engine, but didn't remove the key straight away leaving the lights dimmed, the car's media system illuminated and the music still active. The car had automatically connected to his mobile's music library, as it always did, but George hadn't paid any attention to the tunes on this trip. He couldn't remember one song, or any part of the journey for that matter. He knew the way and must have just made the turns and followed the road subconsciously. George checked his watch. 01:17 am. George figured the road would have been deathly quiet anyway. 'Deathly', he almost laughed at himself, but didn't. He removed the key, turning off the music. What had been playing? He didn't know, he still hadn't paid attention.

With the car lights off, his eyes slowly began to adjust to the moonlight, which was plentiful on this cloudless night. He'd come to a stop right in front of the coastal path he'd walked so many times before, alone at first and then with Sarah and only with Sarah from that point onwards. Just him this time though. Just George. He felt a rising, swelling pressure in his chest as his eyes began to tear up, but he was tired of tears so undid his seatbelt and got out of the car in a hurry. The frigid night air bit at his scalp immediately and the breeze crept between the gaps of his shirt buttons. He opened the car's rear door and grabbed his long jacket and beanie. Once wrapped up, he locked the car and set off along the trail under the veil of night.

The moon did a brilliant job of lighting the way and George considered himself lucky. He hadn't thought about bringing a torch. Practical matters weren't high up on his priority list. He figured he could have used his phone's torch but it wasn't the best. After a few minutes walking, George realised he hadn't thought about Sarah or any of his life's troubles for the first time in a long time. The elements and trail by twilight had provided a welcome distraction. Perhaps they would make the task at hand that little easier, too. With that, sadness returned and engulfed him like a cold, heavy blanket. He sighed, rubbed his teary eyes and continued along the path trying to subdue his thoughts. He knew the spot he was looking for, it wasn't far now.

George arrived. The cliff side path at this specific juncture became very rocky. Not small rocks to kick underfoot, but large immovable stones breaking out from the cliff face, overhanging both the path itself overhead, and reaching out on the ocean side offering those brave enough to walk out on it an unobstructed view of the coastline for at least a mile or two in each direction.

George had stood in the precarious spot himself more than once, to strike a pose for Sarah to snap with her camera. No photos this time. No Sarah either. Just George, the ledge and the sea.

George took a deep breath, then calmly stepped off the path and onto the stone platform, slowly edging himself step by step towards the wide rock's hard lip. He peered down to the water below, the sound of agitated waves hitting rocks had grown louder now as the sound of their crack and hiss was carried up the cliff face with the wind. George tried to clear his mind. He'd thought about this moment many times and hoped to find just a little peace before the end. He'd felt that if he could leave just a little of his torment behind, it might aid his passing. A clear head would surely help him find the stillness he sought. No more pain, no more regret, no more bitterness or suffering, just quiet. A quiet mind. A mind at rest. George started to breathe in and out purposefully and deeply to quell the anxiety building in his chest. He could feel his hands and body shaking. Was it the cold or the fear? He wasn't sure, but didn't care. This was the time. This would be the change he was looking for…all it would take was one step further…

"Have you ever seen the moon so bright?"

The voice startled George so much he almost fell off the edge let alone jump. He didn't fall though, he turned to identify the speaker but the path was empty in both directions as far as he could tell.

"Can't say I've ever seen it so bright, but then again maybe I have. Hard to take an accurate measurement with your mind isn't it?" The voice continued in a warm casual manner, as if addressing someone familiar. George didn't move. He knew he wasn't hearing things, but struggled to see the speaker.

"I know it's not the first time I've *thought* the moon was brighter than ever, so maybe it isn't. Maybe it's just the brightest night, since the last bright night. One thing's for sure though, she sure isn't holding any light back for herself. The moon I mean."

"Where are you?" George asked, his tone was cold and defensive.

"Oh, I'm sorry. Didn't mean to scare you. You probably can't see me under here can you?"

A scruffy looking black man, with a wild beard but bright eyes, stepped out from the darkness under the overhanging cliff rock. His clothes were tatty, but he was layered up to protect himself from the cold.

"It goes back further than you think. Makes a pretty good shelter you know. Not bad tonight but when it rains this here is the best place to be. Even the floor stays dry. I spotted that straight away, the stone and dirt under here's bone dry. Nothing worse than a damp bed, believe me. Makes keeping the cold out so much harder."

George tried to deal with the flood of emotions he was feeling. He was embarrassed and irritated at the same time. He'd planned and considered this in his head a hundred times and never dreamt he'd meet anyone at this time of night in such a remote place.

"Sorry to disturb you. I thought about keeping quiet but you didn't just walk past. Most do. Then you lingered and I figured the longer I waited to say something the ruder I'd seem when I did so, yeah, here I am. Oh, I'm Chris by the way."

George realised he was clenching his teeth and forced himself to relax his jaw.

"I'm George." He paused for a beat then decided to force a brief smile to seem normal.

"Nice to meet you, sir. Nice to meet you. I wasn't expecting to see anyone this late, but a bit of conversation's always welcome."

George considered his options. He couldn't very well jump now that Chris was with him. Not here at least. This wasn't the plan at all. He could walk further along but then it wouldn't be the place he'd planned. Did that matter? He imagined it shouldn't, but it did.

"I wasn't expecting to see anyone out here, Chris." George said, trying to hide the annoyance in his voice.

"I prefer the quiet. It's a beautiful spot. Dry like I said, shielded from the wind and no one tells me to move on out here. I'm not in the way of anything." Chris said positively, then walked out to join George on the stone ledge. "And just look up."

George looked up at the night sky and took in the plethora of stars above him.

"Don't get me wrong," Chris continued. "It ain't perfect for stars tonight what with the moon being so loud and all, but still, it's pretty magical isn't it? In town you never see many stars, just the few brightest ones. It's the light pollution you see, but I don't need to tell you that. I can see you're a smart gentleman." Chris pointed at George's long black woollen pea coat. "Yeah, I spend a lot of time looking at the sky. With no roof over my head I think I'm more like early man, you know what I mean? They knew more about the sky than we did I reckon. They'd use it to navigate, measure time, calendars and stuff, all sorts. I think before electricity people had a better connection with the world and our place in it."

George smiled a genuine smile. "You're getting pretty deep, Chris."

Chris peered over the edge. "Long way down. Not sure how deep the water is but it sure looks *cold*. This moonlight makes it look even colder doesn't it? The white crests of the waves shine so crisply it looks like arctic ice smashing the rocks down there. Not in the summer though. Standing here in the sunshine under a blue sky feels like you're on the edge of the world, looking out at a sea of possibility. You can just imagine the adventures to be had."

George felt the sadness swell again. He'd hoped to have many adventures of his own with Sarah. She'd moved on now and there was no going back. His job had gotten in the way and now that was gone, too. Now his only adventure was loneliness.

"Why are you out here, Chris? If you don't mind me asking?"

"You mean how long have I been homeless? About 16 years. By choice mind, by choice. I had a job, family for a while. Working, coming home, working coming home, bills, bills, bills, until once my kids were older and the wife left me then I wondered what was the point? So here I am. My own man. I got some money saved too. May buy myself a camper one day, but for now, I'm comfortable and unlike you…" Chris reached into his coat pocket and pulled something out, "I've got a torch."

Chris shone the torch at the rock face, lifting the darkness to reveal his mini snug under the big rock. "I've got everything I need right there. I was lacking a bit of convo but now I've got you." Chris laughed.

"What about your kids? Do they know where you are?"

"Sure. I keep in touch. See 'em every now and then. They think I'm crazy, but I don't care. I'm happy."

"Good for you, Chris. I wish everyone could be so happy."

"Troubles?"

"Ha," George couldn't keep the hollow laugh in. "I'm a mess, mate. Haven't been right for a while. This is actually the first time I've left the house apart from work."

George couldn't believe he'd said it out loud. He'd never told anyone how he was feeling and yet here he was telling a complete stranger on a cliff face in the middle of the night.

"Well, whatever the problem, getting out's important, so important. You have to. When you're stressed or feeling down you need to see life carrying on around you." Chris was animated and full of energy. "The sun goes down, but it comes up again. Birds still sing their songs, it rains and it stops, clouds block the sun, then they pass. This is real life, the nature that's all around us. Work will suck you dry. Believe me. If you weren't happy in the job then losing it was a gift."

George thought a moment then found words flowing out his mouth.

"I thought I was happy, Chris. Had a fiancée and a good job. My salary kept rising and rising but with it so did my responsibilities. Kept me away more and more until my girl...Sarah..." George began to well up again. "She err...she left me. I was devastated, but told myself I still had a good job and prospects. You know, a lot to offer. But it didn't take long to realise I only wanted her. She'd moved on by then and not long after...I was made redundant." George wiped his tears and laughed. "I can't believe I'm telling you all this. The last thing you need is to hear all my moaning. I haven't even told my mum."

"What would your mum say?" Chris asked.

George pondered a second. "She'd probably just give me a hug and tell me to come home for a while."

"Don't you like hugs then?" Chris joked.

George paused.

"Yeah, I do. I like hugs." He smiled, "You're pretty easy to talk to Chris, I'll give you that."

"I used to be a therapist."

"Really?" George asked, surprised.

"No." Chris laughed again, clearly tickled. "Hold on."

Chris, pulled out his torch again and shone it on the ground around him searchingly until he found an egg sized rock and picked it up.

"Here, take this." Chris put the rock in George's hand. "Do you know what that is?"

George looked at the rock in his hand.

"A rock." George answered tentatively.

"No, it's bullshit." Chris stated.

George looked at him quizzically.

"All the bullshit in your life, everything crap that's happened to you is right there in your hand. Work bullshit, relationship bullshit, life's bullshit, all of it. There it is!"

George stared at the uneven, cold, dirty stone in his palm.

"Now what are you going to do with it? Carry it around with you? Hold on to it everywhere you go? No, throw it away. Go on. Take the bullshit and throw that into the sea!"

George paused and stared at the rock processing Chris's message.

"Come on. Throw it away. You don't need it!"

George turned to face the sea, rock still in hand. It couldn't be that simple could it? Yet, this random guy living on a cliff face was making so much sense. He was so alive and George wanted some of this guy's energy and positivity. George took a long scornful look at the rock and pulled back his arm before launching it out over the cliff edge and into the choppy water below. He didn't hear it splash but didn't care. It felt good. He felt good. Still emotional, still hurting and hardly on top of the world but amazingly and importantly, he didn't feel hopeless.

"Thank you, Chris." George had never said those words

more sincerely in his life. "That felt really good."

"I didn't do anything. You threw it, not me." Chris smiled.

George smiled gratefully. "I'm pleased to have met you, even under these circumstances."

"Well, what's that I can see in your beard?" Chris asked quickly, changing the subject and pointing to George's short cut facial hair.

George touched his face curiously then realised what Chris was getting at. "Are you referring to my ginger beard, Chris?" He smiled. "I've heard them all before, mate." George joked.

"Nah, you misunderstand me. Take ginger and shuffle the words around. What else can you spell?"

George thought for a moment puzzled. He guessed a joke was coming but couldn't figure it out.

"Can't work it out?"

George shook his head.

"N-word. I'm telling you it's no joke. Gingers and n.....s, we've been persecuted for years! We've got to stick together." Chris winked and George laughed out loud.

They laughed together for a moment then George held out his hand. "You're crazy, but thank you again."

"Gotta be slightly bonkers to live on a path next to that drop." Chris replied grasping George's hand. "So, what now?"

"I don't know. I guess, I'll head back to the car and take it from there. Maybe I'll call my mum in the morning."

"Good man, good man. Go get that hug!"

"Doesn't feel right leaving you here on your own though."

"Don't fret it. I'm fine. I told you, I'm happy.."

George hesitated. "Will you be here for long?"

"I think so. No plans to go anywhere yet."

"The view hasn't tempted you to go on an overseas adventure then."

"Nah. I was born here. This land's my adventure. Let others have theirs."

"Well, maybe I'll come back and chat again some time?"

"Do. Tell me about the hug. Maybe not in the middle of the night though, eh?" Chris joked. "Oh, and bring something good to eat. Anything you like, surprise me, I'm not fussy." Chris laughed.

"I will, Chris. I will."

And he did. Frequently.

They never directly discussed what they both knew George had planned that night, they didn't need or care to. Time had moved on and their friendship, while born from it, seemed to have a meaning far greater. George had always thought *angels* were sent to rescue people, not random guys living on a narrow path hugging the coast called Chris. Chris didn't have wings, but he had a heart of gold, an indomitable spirit and a unique view of the world. The association stuck though. George could never speak of anything religious or remotely spiritual without remembering *his* angel called Chris. So, when others would go to church, George, well, George would visit Chris, to talk, philosophise and just sit...on a narrow path, at the edge of the world, looking out at a sea of possibilities.

The Homeless Poltergeist

A Lorne Turner Short Story by Joe Talon

This story is a standalone, but for fans, it takes place after The Alchemist's Corpse, the sixth book in the Lorne Turner Supernatural Thriller series.

The phone rang, and I jerked awake with a grunt. The fire glowed, looking sullen in the last of the daylight from the sitting room's big window. Despite the bright spring day, the moor remained chilly.

I grabbed the phone. "Turner."

Silence for a moment. "You alright?"

"Ella." I hadn't glanced at the screen properly and I'd missed the name of my closest friend. "Yeah, fine. What's up?"

"You sure you're okay? You sound odd." She worried, but I'd figured out a long time ago it came with the territory of being a vicar.

"Sure, I'm fine." Then I reconsidered. She'd only keep on if I didn't cough up the truth. "Nightmare last night. Heather needs her sleep, so I went for an early run. I dozed off in front of the fire. Don't tell her." Early run being code for: 04:45 run to chase away the endless rattle of the .50cal machine gun in my head.

"Okay. Well, you know where I am if you need to talk about it."

That's one of the things I loved about Ella. The offers of help came with an edge of practicality. She knew the dreams were worse again, but she also knew I'd ask for help when I was ready and not before. In the meantime, she'd check in with me to ensure I remained sane.

"Now we've established I'm still in the land of the living. What can I do for you?" I asked.

Her doubt leaked over the phone long before she spoke. "Can you leave Stoke Pero for a few days?"

"In theory, why?" My mind ran through all the things I'd need to do before leaving the farmhouse.

"There's a problem down in Cornwall and I could do with some help."

"The cathedral need storming?" I asked, trying to lighten the sombre mood in her voice.

She managed a forced chuckle. "It's not the soldier I need. Well, I hope it isn't." Again, I heard the frown in her words. "I need some help in the context of my Deliverance Consultancy."

I paused. Ella and I had worked together on several paranormal problems, but I tried to stay out of her work as an exorcist. Besides, if it was Cornwall, the problem was far out of her diocese.

I'd waited too long.

"No," she said. "I shouldn't be asking. You're busy with the business and Heather and the dog and—"

"Of course, I'll help." It would take some fast talking with Heather to square it away, but once I said Ella needed help, we'd figure it out. "When do you need me?"

"Don't you want to know what the problem is?" she asked.

"I'm guessing it has something to do with people being scared by bumps in the night?"

"Well, there are bumps, that's for certain. I'm actually down in Plymouth right now. Could you come today?"

I checked my watch. "It's 14:50." I did some fast calculations in my head. It would take longer to explain to Heather than to pack for an overnight. "I can be with you by 17:00 depending on traffic. I'll come down on the bike." The drive down, despite having to wiggle around Exeter, would be lovely during the spring afternoon. We didn't have any rain forecast for several days.

We finalised plans and Ella sent me the address. I rang Heather and explained I might be away for a day or so with Ella. Other than missing out on a potential adventure, she was fine about it. During the spring, her work became all-consuming with the Exmoor National Park Authority.

Within twenty minutes, I was on the road and heading towards the big city.

The address Ella gave me turned out to be the Minster Church of Saint Andrews. I saw her small RAV4 parked in the cobbled lane and drew up behind her. Other than the large gothic medieval church, the area looked like service industry central. Every building appeared to be dedicated to moving paperwork, money and people's lives around. The squat concrete and glass buildings fixed forever in the decade classy architecture forgot; that of the nineteen seventies. Still, there were green spaces and trees around the noble church, rising like a stone angel among concrete demons.

Ella hopped down from a wall. I pulled my bike helmet off and rubbed my naked scalp free of sweat. The diminutive figure of my friend made me feel like a giant, a rare illusion. I'm not a big bloke, which meant she felt small.

"Thanks for coming down," she said, a slight apology in her hazel eyes.

"No problem. What's up?"

She ran a hand through her short salt and pepper hair, more salt these days, and sighed. "It's a weird one. I'm here because, well, no one else really wanted to deal with it. I'm one of the few Deliverance Consultants in the South West who's also worked in a challenging urban environment."

Before she became a vicar in the idyllic village of Luccombe on Exmoor, Ella had worked in some scary places in South London. Her time with addicts and sex workers helped to change lives, but she now loved the challenges of her rural parish. We had our problems on the moor with county-lines drug gangs, rural poverty and lack of care for the elderly. It certainly kept her busy.

We headed towards the wall and sat.

She gathered her thoughts for a moment. "From what I can gather, it all started during the winter. Stonehouse isn't the best area of the city, but these people have tried to build a sort of community in a squat in Hick's Lane." A hand waved in the general area she meant.

"Okay, well, I'm guessing there is something spooky living in an old house?"

Ella rarely needed prompting when we talked about the supernatural. Since I'd come to terms with the weird things I saw, and managed to differentiate them from my PTSD, we'd done some good work together and had trust.

"Yes. I hope it's just an imprint of something in the house, but people are scared and this community is isolated and ignored."

"What do you need from me?" I asked, concerned by the level of worry in her hazel eyes.

"I might need some muscle. There're a few addicts living in the place, some of them ex-Navy."

"Marines?" I asked.

Her eyes, full of sympathy, gave me the confirmation I needed. I cursed. Too many men like me ended up on the streets. If it hadn't been for Ella, the bank might well have taken the farmhouse I'd inherited from my debt burdened father, and I'd be here as well. She'd helped to keep my head on straight those first few years after I'd left The Regiment. Twenty years of enjoying the delights of the War on Terror did bad things to a man. I'd never regret my service, never, but it left just as many scars on the inside as I carried on the surface.

"Okay, I can handle them," I said. "What else?"

"There's a young family. Just before Christmas, their landlord hiked up their rent. They couldn't meet the mortgage payments any more with the latest interest rate rise."

22

I knew that terror. Heather and I were struggling again, having just managed to get straight.

Ella continued, "They earned too much between them to get the right benefits or to gain social housing. So, with two teenage girls, they're squatting in this old Victorian house full of scary men with drug and trauma problems."

"Can't they rent somewhere else?" I asked.

She shook her head. "Have you seen how much rents have gone up? Jay lost his job as a security guard when the company realised he didn't have a proper address. Colleen is a nurse and just doesn't earn enough to keep it all together. They had debts, so can't get a credit rating for a housing agency." Her hands went up in frustration. "It basically trapped them in a poverty cycle that's dragging them down. Then there's the others in the building. Wicky, he's a heroin addict who screams most nights about gunfire in Sangin. Basil Brush, who is a real sweetheart, tries to keep him quiet, but he's an alcoholic... Then others come and go, some of them scaring the girls. Though Basil is stopping random people from staying these days."

"Basically, it's bad."

"Yes. The guys in the place, they try to be good for the kids. Jay knew them because his old job did security work at the local pub. They are desperate. All of them. Then some weird things happened."

"We need to go see the place. Maybe do that before you tell me what's going on. I'll be free of preconceived notions."

She nodded. "Thanks." A small hand squeezed my arm. "I'm glad you're here."

"We're a ghost busting team, Ella," I said, with a grin, trying to keep the mood light.

We jumped off the wall and walked to the old RAV.

Hick's Lane and Looe Street had some pleasant houses and pubs. It also had the squat. An old Victorian building three storeys high stood out like a boil on a parson's nose. The once glossy black paint and fine brickwork now looked embarrassed by its dilapidated state. The narrow alley alongside the house, led to a carpark and what looked like a modern single storey add-on to the back of the house. A condemned notice hung off a metal fence and graffiti, far removed from the Banksys in the city, added the only colour to the fouled grey surface and boarded-up rear windows.

The sun was setting in a sullen orange and I caught the waft of the nearby harbour under the car fumes. Trees, their branches kissed by spring, tried to lighten the energy of the area, but I doubted even the most optimistic person could find pleasure in this small, dank, and forgotten corner of the city.

"This way," Ella said, sliding between the wall and the metal gate covered in 'Keep Out' notices.

We picked our way through the rubble of broken bathroom porcelain, bricks from a slowly dissolving Victorian garden wall, rampant lilac bushes, and the ever present plastic bottles. These being for cider rather than water. We both carried shopping bags full of food, cleaning equipment, and I noticed sanitary products. Heather had once explained about period poverty—not a conversation I wanted to have again—but until I'd lived with her, I didn't know how much it cost to keep yourself clean as a woman. You learn a lot about the normal world when you leave the army.

Ella walked up to a metal door that someone had obviously put in place to prevent squatting. She banged hard. I realised, whoever opened this place, made certain not to do damage to the entrance. Criminal damage gave the authorities an excuse to arrest people. No damage, and the owners would have to start eviction proceedings. Or that's what I thought happened. Once more, my walking encyclopaedia of the underworld, Heather, had explained it to me once after we'd been in a squat in Minehead. We'd been looking for an addict who'd helped some Russian mercenaries murder an old lady on behalf of an American drug company. Sometimes, my quiet retirement turned out to be more dangerous than the work I did in The Regiment.

I glanced up at the tall building and on a piece of fallen gutter a jackdaw balanced. The pale eyes watched me, curiosity obvious.

The door opened from the inside and a woman stood haloed by candlelight.

"Hi Colleen," Ella said, in her warm-blanket vicar voice.

The woman's face crumbled as she fought not to cry. "You came back." She had deep brown eyes, stained even darker by the black suitcases of sleepless nights and the hollow cheeks of a woman who wasn't thin by choice. Her mousy hair, though, was clean and done up in a tidy ponytail. She wore a hospital uniform.

"Of course I did, and I have help. Come on. I've some food for the kids."

I lifted the bags I carried. "Hello. I'm Lorne." The jackdaw launched itself into the air with a clarion cry for the dead. He'd be reporting back to his family about the lack of food in the scruffy garden.

Colleen stepped back from the door. "It's, um, well…"

Ella slipped through the narrow gap and I squashed in, the door not opening fully. Colleen's candle filled the dim interior with crazy shadows. They leaped and crawled over old flock wallpaper. We stood in a room that might once have opened onto the delights of a kitchen garden and gentle lawn. Now it looked and smelt rotten. A scurrying sound made Colleen flinch.

I said, "I hope the rats here are smaller than the ones in Lashkar Gah. Them buggers will have an ear off given a chance." I added a heavy twist to my Somerset accent, softening the sentiment.

It worked. She chuckled. "These'll only take a toe."

"Pfft, they're just babies then."

"You served?" she asked.

"Yes, ma'am. I hear you live with some comrades?" I followed the candle as it danced ahead of us.

"Wicky and Basil were both Marines. They found each other on the streets a while back and opened the squat last winter. They are good boys, even if they have their problems. We're using this room as a kitchen. It's cleaner than some of the others on the ground floor," she said, ushering us into a smaller room.

We walked through a narrow hall, past the stairs, and took a right into a front room. The windows weren't boarded up, but little daylight now remained in the sky.

Colleen's hands twisted as we set the bags on a spotless Formica table. "We have the water connected, but they won't give us electric or mains gas." A slight flare of light from a passing car. "But we've grown used to the tilly lamps, camping lights and bottled gas for the cooker. The cold baths are a problem, but my boss at work lets us use the showers there and we have the public pool nearby."

"It can't be easy," I said. The feeling of a black feather being dragged over my scalp and down my spine made me turn just as a bang shot through the quiet of the house.

Ella started and let out a small yelp. Then she gave an embarrassed, "Sorry."

"The girls are doing their homework upstairs. Or they're trying to. It's not easy without a computer. They use my phone mostly." Colleen hardly reacted to the sound.

"Where's Jay?" Ella asked.

"At the council. He's been there all day, every day, this week. He won't leave the waiting area of the housing department. Silent protest. I wish he'd spend the time at the job centre, but he says he can do that online as well." She chuckled. "He uses their free wi-fi to hassle them and job hunt. To be honest, I don't have time to worry about him as well. Not right now."

Another bang came from upstairs and a girlish voice shouted at something.

I shivered. "What's happening?"

26

Colleen's eyes shone too brightly in the shallow light and the shadows behind her gathered together in a pack. I wanted to step back.

She said, "I think we have a poltergeist." The obvious exhaustion in her voice made it tight and precise. Colleen was delivering a fact, not asking my permission to believe in something so strange.

I glanced at Ella.

She gave a small shrug. "I know I can banish it," she said. "But, to be honest, it might be easier on everyone if you could tell us more clearly what we're dealing with."

My peculiar talents often made it easier for her to deal with simple spectral oddities.

Colleen went through the bags. "Oh, Ella, you remembered." She held a bag of natural liquorice bears. "They're Rosie's favourites."

Ella smiled. "And there're some flapjacks for Michele."

The hairs on my arms, or those still growing between the burn scars, stood as if on a parade ground. Another bang.

"Mum!" came down the stairs.

I was moving before being completely aware of it. Running for the stairs, I took them two at a time, heading for the landing. Shadows converged on my position, their slick coolness reminding me of a haunted house, now a burned ruin, in the village of Scob.

"Rosie? Michele?" I called out.

A small scream, more banging. I ran down the hall. A dim light leaked under a doorway, straining to escape, to fill the hall. I knocked on the door. "Rosie? Michele? My name is Lorne Turner. I'm here to help. Can I come in?"

"She won't let you," came the scared voice of a young adult.

I tried the door. The brass knob was cold. I twisted, but the door didn't budge.

Colleen and Ella arrived behind me.

The nurse looked ready to faint. "This, it... Why is it doing this in daylight? It's always at night and never this bad."

I glanced at Ella. "Yeah, that could be us."

Ella muttered, "I wanted more time before we started this."

"You did your preliminaries at the church?" I asked.

She nodded.

I sucked in a breath. Old carpet, cold air, the bitter scent of stale drugs and booze, but also the floral taste of furniture polish, scented soap and clean bedding. Focusing on my breathing, I pulled together the blue and white bubble I'd learned to use for protection. I'd prefer some Kevlar body armour, but it never worked against spooks, only bullets.

Slowly, knowing it'd render me unconscious if it backfired, I placed my hand on the door. I whispered, "If you want to talk, I'm right here."

It still baffled me as to how I'd become a powerful psychic since almost dying in Syria. I'd always had a heightened sixth sense for trouble, which had saved the lives in my unit more times than any of us could remember. Then, one day, we'd been trapped in a town on the border with Iraq. ISIS rushed through the place and if they had caught us…

I pushed the memories away. They wouldn't help today. "Come on, talk to me." The spirit needed to meet me halfway or this would turn nasty.

The door swung open violently. I almost fell through. Instead, I stumbled inside. Two girls sat on a small sofa, holding hands. Camping lights gave both children a soft glow. One had green eyes, the other brown. They had the same mousy blonde hair as their mother.

A book lifted off the table and rushed towards my head. Years of training took over, and I twisted off the line. The book hit the wall with a thud that made me glad it missed.

"Stop it," I snapped. "That's just bad manners. I'm trying to help."

The energy in the room flattened. Both girls took a breath.

I looked around the large bedroom, now a living room, and

saw the remains of a family life in a nice home with nice things. A few of the boxes stacked against the wall looked empty, but most still held the possessions the family owned, but didn't want unpacked.

In the corner, by the remains of a Victorian cast iron fireplace, I saw a thicker shadow.

I chose not to focus on it just yet. "Hello ladies. That was a drama. How are you both?"

They glanced at their mum, who stood behind me.

"Come on, girls, let's get out of here. Mr Turner and the Reverend Morgan are going to help." Colleen held out her hand and the girls, giving me one last and fearful look, ran to their parent.

"Clearly I'm scarier than the ghost," I muttered.

Ella chuckled. "What's happening here?"

"Heather would know for sure, but I think we have a severe case of two teenagers in enough emotional distress to unsettle an already unsettled house. Do you agree?" I kept my back to the shadow in the corner, though I felt it gathering strength. An intense electric charge with a sudden drop in temperature.

Ella breathed out hard, and the air misted. Her eyes widened. "We should do a full historical investigation of the house. Find out who owned it, what happened in it, who or what might be doing this."

"Or we could just make it leave. This family is suffering enough. They can't spend another night with banging doors and shaking beds. Then there's the pea soup vomit."

Ella laughed. "Heather's made you watch the Exorcist."

"Watch it? The bloody woman made me read it and Rosemary's Baby. The films were bad enough." I shuddered. "I thought she loved me." This came out as a plaintive murmur.

Ella laughed again, but it was strained this time. "You're right. We have to do this tonight, now. They need some peace. The living and the dead."

I nodded. Ella's sense of the *otherness* in our world hovered slightly above average. She sensed things others didn't, and it made her a good Deliverance Consultant. Her natural empathy for places and people meant she often picked up on the unspoken and drew layers of truth out of people who asked for the Church's help with reluctance.

Me? I shone like a bloody lighthouse to all things weird. I rarely knew what I was doing, and I'd been told more than once I was a tank trampling through psychic realms.

To be honest, I was only now coming to terms with all this old bollocks and would still retreat into denial, given a chance. I often longed for simpler days when I carried a SIG as my sidearm and a L119A1 carbine slung over my chest.

I closed my eyes, reinforced my bubble of protection, threw it around Ella as well, even though she had one of her own, and turned back to the scary corner. It never came easy this part. I never knew what I'd see, and I'd seen some terrible things.

In this instance, it was just a girl, about the age of Colleen's eldest daughter. She stood in the corner with a rounded belly.

"Oh, God," whispered Ella.

My gifts often gave those around me the ability to see what I saw.

The girl wore a uniform that reminded me of the few glimpses I'd seen of Downton Abbey, the servants, not the posh lot. Her hair looked unkempt and ragged. The dress dirty and torn. The belly huge and heavy.

She shivered with the cold and her face had the pinched look of genuine hunger.

Ella whispered, "Do you think she was a servant here?"

"I think she was knocked up by someone living here and tossed out on the street. Or that's what's coming through." I didn't hear words, just a series of images. The girl was the niece of the cook and came from a farm on Dartmoor. She didn't remember what year, but it was after the Great War. She worked in the kitchen, then in the main part of the house. When the son took an interest, she succumbed to his charms, thinking she might marry him one day. It didn't happen.

The moment the family realised she was pregnant, they threw her out. The girl's family maintained a strict religious life on the moor, so she couldn't go home. No one would take her in and when her belly grew too big to hide, she couldn't work as a whore on the nearby docks. The child came, they both died. She left this world cursing the man who'd abandoned her.

The images I drew from the shadow in the corner showed me that he'd gone mad. Whether because of her or syphilis, I didn't know, but the effect was the same. The family died out within a generation. She'd been in the house ever since, looking for release. Having Rosie and Michele here at last, she could reach out using their desperation, unhappiness and fear of an unknown future as a catalyst.

I told Ella all this as the images bombarded me. With two teenagers, the same age as this lost soul in the house and just as homeless, the spectre had found the energy to manifest and demonstrate her terrible grief.

Ella wept for the girl. I stood, silent, a witness to her torment, swallowing my grief as I'd done a thousand times in desert villages while women and children suffered.

I wondered how much had really changed in a century. Nothing for the better in the places where I'd fought. Maybe, nothing here in this modern small European city, one of those we'd shed blood to protect.

Ella prayed. First the oldest Celtic prayer of exorcism, St Patrick's Breastplate, then the Lord's Prayer. Both asking the spirit to move on, to find God, to find forgiveness and to release her hold in this world. Then, using my description of what had happened in this house, she blessed the room and gave the young woman a personal prayer of devotion and love. I followed where I could and offered private prayers to the unhappy spirit so she'd feel able to move on.

Each time a trapped spirit left our world, it came differently. On this occasion, the energy in the room and the vision in the dark corner, eased into softer, kinder shadows. As if the ink were fading on a piece of vellum, so it was clean, ready for a new story to be told.

When Ella finished sprinkling her holy water about, the entire house looked lighter. Not any prettier, but the corners weren't as dark and the ceilings didn't glower.

By the time we finished, Colleen had cooked for the girls, Jay and the ex-Marines. The evening turned into a bit of a party and I swapped a few of the more sanitary war stories with Wicky and Basil Brush—he had a wealth of wiry red hair—before Ella talked them all into joining together for a full blessing and Eucharist.

We left them at around 02:30.

As we walked back to the little RAV, I asked, "Is there anything we can do for them? All of them?"

Ella shrugged. "I'm going to reach out to the Royal British Legion and ask them to help with Wicky and Basil for a start. The problem is they're both addicts. It'll limit the options and be tough, but I'm not giving up. As for the family…"

"It's not easy."

"No."

Three weeks later, while I dug over a new vegetable patch Heather wanted rather than the large lawn, Ella called.

"Hey, guess what?" she sounded full of excitement.

"What?" I asked.

"We've done it. We've found Colleen and the others accommodation. They've a new house on a new estate. Wicky and Basil are in sheltered housing as well."

A huge lump formed in my throat. I coughed manfully, trying to dislodge it. Ella, Heather, our dog Ghost and me, we'd all gone down over the last few weeks to bang on doors and 'get shit done'.

"Well, that's," I swiped at my eyes, "that's good news."

"Yeah, we're all invited to their first barbeque. The girls are overwhelmed. It'll be the first time they've not had to share a room."

I thought back to the vision of the lost girl.

Things were better now, I had to admit it, even on my most jaded days. Our social conscience far surpassed that of previous generations. I'd been in many a 'civilised' country with good social care that had fallen apart because of war. The Syria I'd first seen twenty years ago no longer existed. It didn't take much, only enough people ignoring the bad stuff, for a society to breakdown. For the vulnerable to become lost, alone, homeless and scared. I felt like we always lived on the edge of social chaos, and what marked us as better and more enlightened than previous generations, was not how many dream catchers we owned or how much yoga we practiced, but how much we helped those who needed it most.

I said, "It feels good to have made a difference. To have a win." And for once I hadn't had to shoot anyone, though it came close a few times in the council offices.

"Yeah," Ella said just as softly. "It's good to win for a change."

I hung up as Heather came home from work. When I told her the news, we took a couple of beers up to Dunkery Beacon and toasted our good fortune as the dog chased the swifts in the soft evening light.

Dispossessed

By Helen Hollick

They pulled the house down.

All right, I agree, it *was* old; slates were missing from the scullery roof, the thatch was worn with gaping holes in places. Even the mice had abandoned that thatch, and the bats had moved on long ago. None of the windows closed properly – it wasn't a draught that came in through those ill-fitting frames, but a howling gale, even when there wasn't much wind. The chimney smoked. The floor tiles were cracked and uneven, and the oak rafters were riddled with woodworm. What can you expect? The house was built in the early 1600s. It had witnessed the soldiers trooping to and fro along the valley below: Cromwell's New Model Army and King Charles' Royalists. Aye, and the old house had heard that sound, louder than the boom of thunder when the gunpowder, stored in the crypt beneath the church over Torrington way, had ignited while battle between the two armies had raged outside. Many a good man, on both sides of that dreadful conflict of religious belief, had died that sad, sorry day.

The house had its memories, as do I. It was old, that house, old, like me. But to pull it down? Reduce it to nothing but a pile of dust and rubble? Ah, shame on them.

It had been a lovely house, full of love and laughter. Did they not know that old houses have a soul? That the echoes of the past are captured between the walls, are sealed beneath the roof? If they had stopped long enough to listen they would have heard those echoes, that laughter, that love. The cries of the newborn safely delivered from the womb, the joy of children playing on a sun-baked day, or huddled around the table in the kitchen, their hands, feet and faces turned towards the great open fire. Eager for Mother to stir the pot suspended over the flames and serve the bubbling broth within into earthenware dishes. To smell the mouth-watering aroma of fresh-baked bread. To smear new-churned butter and sweet, sweet honey on thick-cut slices.

Harsh words, too, oft times spoken when patience frayed. What families did not share the occasional tempest? Chores not done, bones weary from hard work, worry gnawing at heart and mind? Aye, angry words spoken, but usually quickly forgiven and forgotten. Although, not always. I smile at the memory: Mother would complain so, when the menfolk trooped into her clean kitchen with mud or cow-slurry on their boots. She appreciated the jugs of fresh milk brought in, though. We, in turn, appreciated the cream she made. The butter, the cheese...

They pulled the chimney down first. Three feet thick it was, with the old bread oven nested beside the fireplace. I sat and watched them do the deed, although they had no idea I was there. I kept myself hidden, for the house was no longer mine. They tore down what had been *my* house, *my* home. And there was nothing, nothing, I could do to stop the destruction.

Ah! They have found the shoe, and the bones of the cat. I'm not really sure what the shoe meant, nor the cat's bones, but it was the expected thing to do when building a house, to seal both in a small cavity within the stones of the chimney. To keep witches at bay, I think. I'd heard it said that the cats were alive when bricked up. Sealed in to die slowly of thirst, hunger and fear. Poor things. Except it wasn't true. A myth. The creature was always already dead.

If the point *was* to keep witches away, it must have worked, for in all the years, I had never seen a witch squinnying around the windows or doors. Never seen a hag spying on the house from the garden, or watching from the dense canopy of the old oak tree.

That had gone as well. The Old Oak. The storm had finally caused its end, blowing it down – right onto the house, which, I suppose, is why they were now demolishing it. The tree had been the final nail in the coffin – *our* coffin, mine and my home's. It had been a splendid great-great – oh, I do not know how many 'greats' – grandfather of an oak. Planted way, way back. Before the defeat of the Armada by Queen Elizabeth, first of that name. Before her father King Hal had sat his fat rump on the throne, and murdered those poor women he'd lusted after. What price a queen's crown, eh?

And the oak had been there before that, when Richard of the White Boar had become king. Had he murdered those nephews of his? Who knew the truth? Only he and their murderer I suppose. If indeed they were slain. Perhaps they'd fled in secret and lived their lives in safe contentment somewhere in exile. If that was the case, had they spent a while homeless, like I am now?

I sit here, concealed within the dense thicket of dogwoods, rose briars and brambles. Yes, brambles; they have not been cleared for many a while, and they do infiltrate so. They had never tended the garden, the people who took my house from me, yet it had, once, been such a beautiful garden. Roses – red and pink and white all with the aroma of Heaven. Blue and purple lavender – which the busy honey bees and fat bumbles so loved. Peonies, foxgloves, violas... As many herbs as you could think of growing in the little walled area set aside for them. Thyme, sage, marjoram, rosemary, cumin, hyssop, rue, dill... All overgrown now, and gone to seed. Swallows had nested every year in the barns, stables and dairy. Along with the house martins, sparrows and little Jenny Wrens. They will need to find new homes now. As will I.

There, it has all gone. Nothing left of my home except an area of spoiled land, ruts and mess. My beautiful home. Gone. The winter was cold, not that I felt the frost, snow and that bitter, bitter north-east wind which blew through every nook, cranny and broken window in the barn where I took what shelter I could. I was too miserable to think of the cold, of fingers too numb to move, of a face frozen like the ice in the stream where the waterfall had become a sculptured cascade. It would all melt when the sun returned. *If* the sun returned. Sometimes, huddled, lonely and I admit, afraid, in the dark of the barn I wondered if the sun would ever shine for me again.

I managed to hide throughout the winter in that old barn – they'd left it standing, and had left the pile of old hay that had been there for years. It was musty, but served its purpose. I shared it with a hibernating dormouse. A barn owl often stared at me from its perch high among the rafters, looking down at me as what little of the winter daylight faded into dusk. I marvelled as it spread its wings and glided, silent as a secret whisper out through the open door and was gone into the night. They used to say that the White Owl was an omen of death, the spirit of one departed. I could well believe it.

There were tawny owls too, out in the woods. A vixen barking to her mate, badgers snuffling for roots, worms and what they could find – finally finishing off what little was left of my garden! When the snow was at its thickest and heaviest the Lords and Ladies of Exmoor came down to forage for what they could find. I heard them often, but only once saw one of them; a stag resplendent in his reddish-brown coat with the spread of his fourth and fifth tines forming into a fitting crown, although his noble appearance was spoiled by the ragged shedding of the velvet. I think he knew I was there, for he stood a long while, head high, as still as a carved statue. Then he moved as fast as lightning flashes, and was gone.

I slept during those long winter months, unaware of what the world was doing outside. Then, with the spring, others came. More noise, more disruption. Banging, clattering, hammering, drilling... I covered my ears and huddled deeper into the dark, concealing shadows of the woods where I now hid. I shut my ears, my eyes, my senses. Shut it all out. This was no longer my home and I cared nothing for them as they cared nothing for me.

I stayed there, safe within the new-grown bracken and uncurling ancient ferns, safe in the dappled shade of the hawthorn, beech, birch and ash. Safe, even when it all stopped and all I could hear was the sound of the leaves, dancing in the wind, and the cows in the valley below, lowing at milking time. The ewes calling, anxious, to their skittering lambs, and the pheasants clucking their absurd cries of alarm. The woods were my home now, and unless – until – they found me and moved me on, here I would stay. Except, one late summer evening I did venture out, just to look. Just *once*, I told myself. I would look just the once to see what these new people had done to my home.

They had rebuilt it. There was the high, sturdy chimney. There was the new thatch, covering arched oak beams. I peeped through a window – new slate flags on the kitchen floor, new cupboards, everything new but in the style of what I had known and loved when this had been my home.

They were a family, Father, Mother, three children – two girls and a boy. Oh, I was pleased about that, my old home needed children to fill it with love and laughter. One of them, the eldest girl by the look of her, glanced up from what she was doing and stared at me peering through the window. I willed her to not shout out, to not draw attention. I put my finger to my lips, *sssh!* Indicating would she stay as quiet as that dormouse in the barn, as silent as that spread-winged angel-owl?

She did not shout, or scream, but smiled at me. I smiled back, nodded.

This used to be my home, I thought. My home, where I had lived and laughed and loved. Would this new family learn to love it as much as I did? I turned away from the window, the sting of tears in my eyes, my heart as heavy as death. This was their home now. Not mine.

Then I heard her voice, the girl's voice, clear in my mind.

I remember a time when that question was nothing to worry about. But now a tightness grows, somewhere in my stomach, it makes me cold, shivery, vulnerable. I can smell the bread. I think I can smell the flour that has dusted the crust. There's a sharp tang of raw onion too. I take the bag, hold it as though it might explode. There is cheese. It was my go-to sandwich when I was studying at college, my whole life ahead of me. Is it chance? How would he know to bring me that?

I ease the sandwich out of the bag. Dark yellow cheese, white onion, fresh white bread. When I take a bite, I travel back in time. A world without Tom. My throat won't let me swallow. I want to scream and cry at the same time. Crazy woman. Druggy. Scrounger. I know that's what people would think if I screamed.

"I remember how you always used to be eating cheese and onion sarnies, all the time."

He was still next to me. His body an echo of mine, elbows resting on his knees. He knows me. We are both looking straight ahead. I've forgotten how to look at someone, maybe he doesn't want to look at me, not how I am. I have to ask.

"Do you know me?"

He doesn't answer. I turn to look at him as he turns to look at me. He has a beard, I didn't notice that before, and pale blue eyes.

"Mark?" I ask.

He laughs. Not unkindly. "Didn't know if you'd remember me."

"Your shoes are muddy." It was the only thing I could think to say. In my head it was an acknowledgement of trust.

"Yep. They are muddy. You're right there."

I looked back at my sandwich, trying to make a connection between it, and Mark, and where I was.

"I run an outdoor education centre now." He said. "Never really slotted into that whole classroom thing."

He comes from so far in my past that I'd almost forgotten I

43

was that person. She was one who studied because she enjoyed it. She had ambition, maybe even a vocation. She got married, was thinking about a family. Stupid. Stupid. Stupid. That was when it all crumbled. He didn't want a family.

"Thanks for the sandwich."

I had to say something, but I'm not used to kindness, not genuine kindness.

"I heard you left Tom. Nobody knew why."

When someone punches you in the stomach, causes a miscarriage, it doesn't make sense to hang around.

"What are you doing now?" he asks.

I want to swear at him, ask him what the fuck it looks like I'm doing. I don't. I think. Maybe for the first time in seven months I allow myself to think.

"Waiting." I say, after a time.

He doesn't ask any more personal questions, just sits with me for a while. It's good not feeling alone, but I don't want him to stay, I'm out of practice with people.

"Will you be here tomorrow?" he asks.

I shrug. I don't have plans.

From what I remember, Mark was a bit of a loner at college, never part of the crowd. We spoke a few times. I couldn't say I knew him well. But how well do you know anyone? I married Tom. I thought I knew him.

"I will stop by. Hope to see you."

I've come back to the same spot today, not sure why. Do I really want to see Mark again or am I simply incapable of making changes. By mid-morning I find myself examining walking boots as they approach, looking for ones with a thin green line just above the sole, two-tone laces done up in a double knot.

They stop beside me, and I feel my body tense up, ready to run, but I'm not sure I could if I tried. My life has been lived at a slow pace for months. He has sat down again, offered me a carrier bag.

"Thought you might be able to use these."

I don't want to look in the bag. Will it be some token of a new beginning. This life suits me fine for now, no baggage, quite literally, no commitments, nobody to shit on me.

Desert boots. He's brought me bloody desert boots. I manage to mumble my thanks. He talks for a while. I have no idea what about.

Somewhere inside my head I recognise that I'm living in a kind of never ending loop. There was a time when I had plans that stretched years ahead. By the time I walked out on Tom, I was down to just days ahead, planning meals, making sure everything in the house was how he liked it. Now it's only hours or minutes ahead. I need to escape the loop I'm in.

It was time to move on, a new street, in a new town, and a plan. I know there are people who will help me if I need them. And I probably do. I swapped the boots for a watch. It has a calendar function. Today is Wednesday, the 16th of October. Someone asked me if I needed anything today, and I said a small notebook and a pen. They looked surprised but returned with both items a few minutes later. I can write out a plan now.

It rained today and I wish I didn't have that hole in my shoe. But I could never have worn those desert boots.

But for the Grace of God

by Ian Riddle

It was a dark, dank December day, although, in fairness, the weather was normal for the time of year. Even so, it was still miserable, a day for scarves and gloves, long coats and boots. Days of shorts and summer sandals, not all that long past, were consigned to fading memories and forgotten photographs.

It was also early afternoon, though only the clock on the front of the old civic hall seemed to know that; the low light levels suggested it to be much later. It already had the feel of early evening about it. It had been like that now for several days and was unlikely to improve that side of the solstice. Just about everyone had given up hope of ever seeing any blue again as they moved around, formless, bundled as they were against the cold. Grey was the then current norm.

The one bright spot in all the dark though, was that Christmas was on its way; the decorations in the shop windows and in the air above the streets confirmed it. That was the one positive; at least to most.

It was most definitely a positive to the young woman, intent on starting her Christmas shopping. Although she was currently railing at the work it involved, her husband was being no help, she knew she'd thoroughly enjoy it all the same when the time came. In particular, there was both Christmas morning, watching their young daughter open her presents and Christmas day lunch at her parents to look forward to. On top of all that, there were also the several parties they'd planned to either give or attend.

It was also somewhat uplifting to the old gentleman widowed that spring. The festive feeling that was starting to flow through the streets helped raise his spirits, if only a little, from the low they'd descended to and stayed at following his wife's death.

All this activity though, this hustle and bustle, this playing of carols and Christmas songs, had no effect whatsoever on the fellow sat hunched and huddled on the pavement, the portico above him his only shelter. The nearby doorway to the bank was the best he had to call home at the time and only then after the bank had closed for the night and staff had left. Christmas would be just another cold, miserable and meaningless day to him. It was unlikely he'd notice it.

The main thoroughfare, the High Street, now for the most part pedestrianised, runs north-south through the city, from the bus station at the top of the hill all the way to the river at the bottom. It's dissected, roughly halfway along its route, by another road that cuts across it, running east-west. The main shopping area lies in the top sector, to the north of this bisection. It runs all the way from there to the bus station where, eventually, it starts to peter out as it begins to mix and blur with small city suburbia.

Parallel to the High Street, on the eastern side, is Burrow Street, named after a former Alderman, long dead and once home to the prosperous merchants and city elders. It's still an elegant tree-lined boulevard but now houses the offices of the professional element, the solicitors, the accountants, the private bankers and one or two of the more up-market estate agents.

At the time of telling a young woman, Fiona, a solicitor well on the rise, was leaving the warmth off her office in Burrow Street to join the shopping throng in the High Street.

As always, she was smartly dressed, this time in a blue, pin-stripe suit, the skirt cut just sufficiently above the knee to show her legs to best advantage without, in any way, seeming unprofessional. Her colour-matching heels gave added height. On top of the suit, she sported a three-quarter length, cashmere coat, sash-tied at the waist, its collar turned upwards in protection. Her long blonde hair hung straight and brushed to her shoulders. Her make-up, as always, was immaculate.

Fiona was quite an attractive woman and might even have been considered pretty if she'd ever smiled. She'd rarely ever smiled though, other than to her daughter. Fiona was always far too busy for smiling; she and her husband, Radcliffe, had places to go. Getting there occupied much of their time.

They were an aspirational, late thirties couple; the acquisition of a notable four-wheel drive was in discussion for post-Christmas, when the new number plates would be introduced. Fiona also harboured ambitions to move to a much larger house than their present four-bedroomed one just as soon as funds permitted. She wanted something that would be thought of as more of a 'residence'.

Almost simultaneously with Fiona leaving her office the old gentleman, Albert, was just alighting from a bus at the other end of the High Street to her. He started a steady descent, his speed of walking nowhere matching Fiona's clip-clop, clip clop, as she hurried, purposefully between shops. There was a time when he would once have stridden out, but those days had long gone; his walking speed was now curtailed with age. He'd learned to allow himself plenty of time wherever he was going.

On this particular day, Albert was heading for the patisserie at the lower end of the pedestrianised area. It was very much the opposite end to where the bus had deposited him but that didn't matter. Albert was going out for afternoon tea; it was an occasion and something he'd been looking forward to. Afternoon tea there was something Albert and his late wife had used to do, once in a while.

As this was to be a Christmas treat Albert had dressed appropriately, wearing his best suit, together with his old, but still serviceable, overcoat. Had his wife been alive he knew she would have expected him to have dressed as such. Even after her death, Albert wouldn't have wanted to have disappointed her.

Somewhere, roughly half-way between Fiona's and Albert's starting points was the man sat on the piece of cardboard under the portico. The cardboard was the main thing that separated his backside from the cold of the paving stones. Known to the local, homeless charity only as Tony, he was someone who was probably younger than his face suggested. His situation had exaggerated his aging. Christmas parties and afternoon tea were ideas far from his thoughts; survival was the best he could hope for.

There was nothing designer about Tony's wear either; it wasn't even tidy, swathed in jumpers and an anorak as he was, with the hood pulled up over his head and ears. He was cocooned in a sleeping bag that had seen better days too, as he searched for a warmth he no longer felt. Tony was pretty much oblivious to the world around him. Most of his senses were either dulled or dead.

Tony also tended to keep his gaze to ground level, trying to avoid eye contact. Experience had taught him to avoid unwanted and unwarranted attention. For the most part, the majority of people just ignored him, but there were always those one or two, as he well knew, who could be abusive; some even downright offensive. He remembered being spat on and having both firecrackers set off by his feet and having been urinated on as he'd slept, on more than one occasion.

Fiona was taking a late lunch break. Work was still busy and there were cases she wanted off her desk before the Christmas holidays. It would impress the partners, she knew, and she was starting to angle for a partnership herself. Her husband, Radcliffe, already had his with the firm he worked for. It would be good if the both of them were at that level, Fiona felt; it would also give her mother something else to boast about amongst her circle of friends.

It didn't help Fiona's case, though, at least to her mind, that she was a working mother; it wasn't easy juggling work and home. She just didn't have the time to devote to 'getting on' as Radcliffe had. It had been so much easier for him; all he'd ever done was focus on his job.

Fiona griped to herself. She wished sometimes that he'd undertake his share of domestics and not leave them all to her, as he was doing again now; give her a sporting chance.

Sometimes, Radcliffe could be infuriating. Christmas, Fiona felt, was one of those times. It would be easy for him; all he would have to do would be the perfect host, or guest, depending on the occasion. For Fiona not only did she have to organise the parties but even when they were guests it would be she who had to arrange baby-sitters. Radcliffe might be good as a solicitor but, in her current opinion, he was useless when it came to most other things. Such thinking didn't leave Fiona in the best of moods as she left her office that afternoon; at that point, she was certainly well below average on the festive-feel barometer.

As a labourer, Albert had never earned big money but he, and his wife Doris, had always lived contentedly enough, certainly to their satisfaction. They'd never particularly wanted for anything but, at the same time, they hadn't particularly wanted either, certainly not to any excess. They'd always had sufficient for their needs.

They'd eaten well, kept a comfortable, if modest home, in the Edwardian terrace that they'd lived in for fifty years and had always managed a package tour somewhere each summer. It was never anywhere particularly exotic in the great scheme of things but to them, visiting foreign parts, always brought out an almost childish excitement as they packed and headed for the airport.

Even in retirement things hadn't been all that bad, not whilst there'd been the two of them though there'd been precious little surplus. Now, with his wife dead these past several months, times had become a bit more difficult for Albert and not only from her passing. There was now just the one pension to live on although the bills always seemed, to Albert's mind, as if they were still meant to be for two.

With money now that much tighter and Doris gone, Albert hadn't really been looking forward to Christmas. If anything, he had, in fact, been dreading its coming. It was going to be a funny time, he'd thought, Doris not being there to share it with him. It would be his first Christmas alone. She wasn't even there that day, to share afternoon tea with, and afternoon tea, at this particular patisserie, had been their little extravagance, one which they'd occasionally indulged in, as funds had allowed.

The patisserie had been their favourite haunt, glorious as it was to Doris, with its slightly genteel ambience. The miniscule slices of sandwich, jam and cream scones, various cakes and of course the pot of tea, served with delicate, china cups had always made her feel a little special. Despite any qualms Albert personally had, about going there without her, he'd promised Doris, before she died, that it was a tradition he would keep alive, if only for her sake.

How he was going to afford it with tightened funds was another matter, but a promise was a promise, especially to Doris. He'd carefully managed his money in the weeks running up to Christmas so that, as he ambled along the High Street that day, he had twenty pounds tucked into his waistcoat pocket. He tapped the pocket as he walked; the note was sitting comfortable, safe, and ready for his purchase.

It seemed hard to believe to anyone looking at the pathetic looking relic sitting under the portico that that was the same Tony who had once had a well-paid job, a steady relationship and an active social life. He used to have a surname too although, by this point, he sometimes struggled to remember it.

In Tony's pre-homeless days there'd been a flat in the more fashionable part of the city, a conversion in one of the old warehouses that had once occupied the wharf alongside the river and a highly active social life. With no children Tony and his partner had been able to enjoy the freedom to be out and about most evenings, even if it was little more than an evening with friends, in one of the trendy wine bars that surrounded them. There'd also been spur of the moment jaunts to London and Paris as well, just for the fun.

Tony had been a young and thrusting estate agent once, working in an office just a few doors away from where Fiona's then was. He was one of the rising young professionals who had had the philosophy of 'work hard, play hard'. It was considered good to be viewed as an 'allrounder'. It was the playing hard though that eventually became Tony's undoing. Had he just worked hard he might have been working still.

Tony had been keen not only to keep fit, but to be seen as being the young, athletic type. Part of that, a big part, involved him in playing squash, two, maybe three nights a week after work. It was during one of those sessions a couple of years or so previous that Tony, somehow, had not only managed to slam the ball and his racket into the wall but himself as well, knee first. How it happened he couldn't really remember; it had all happened so quickly. The upshot though, was that he'd damaged a cartilage in his right knee.

It wasn't so much the injury itself that caused Tony his problem but rather the bungled operation that followed. The attempt to repair the damage by surgery failed and left Tony in permanent pain. The only solution was a prescribed painkiller to which he eventually became addicted. Heavy bouts of drinking, initially under the guise of alleviating the pain, only exacerbated the situation. So too did the cannabis that a friend had suggested he try. The odd spliff had turned into one more.

The drugs and the alcohol weren't a good mix. They may have eased the one pain for a while but in return caused his other. Tony's work and personal relationships soon suffered as he spiralled into a toxic mix of depression, insomnia and drug dependency.

Ultimately, Tony lost everything; his job, his girlfriend, his rather fashionable flat and, of course, his friends who disappeared into the ether faster than the phantoms they soon became. Worst of all though, Tony lost himself. His hopes, his dreams, his every pleasure and passion, his every possibility of happiness, everything that defined Tony, as a person, all fled with the rest.

With nothing left, not even his self-respect, Tony ended up on the streets, sleeping in cardboard boxes and doorways in the city centre, forgetting who he was, where he'd come from. With nowhere consistent to stay or sleep, Tony became so tired that he could barely think straight anymore.

Fiona, having left her office, paused only briefly to check her to-do list and mentally calculated a shop-based route that would take her from where she was to the last one on her list at the top end of town as quickly and efficiently as possible. She hadn't time to mess around, she needed to be focused. She still had work to complete and there was her daughter to collect from school.

Fiona dipped and dived in and out of the various shops weaving her way around like-minded people as she progressed. She worked her way steadily up-hill until her bags started to fill with cards and wrappings, little gifts, chocolates and other tasties, all the things in fact that were going to make Christmas so perfect.

Fiona and Albert's paths crossed as they passed Tony. Fiona, immediately judgmental, took one look at him, sitting there, dishevelled and dirty, and physically, gave him a wide berth as if he might be contagious.

"Not another one," she thought. It wasn't right, she felt, that decent people should be affronted this way. It certainly wasn't seemly to have people like him just sitting there, on the pavements, making the place look untidy. It was appalling, absolutely appalling.

"Poor bugger," Albert said to himself, "and I thought I was in for a rough Christmas. It is true what they say, there's always somebody worse off."

As Tony sat, he was at eye level with Fiona's legs. There was a time when he certainly would have noticed them, might even have commented to himself on them. That, however, was another time. These days they were just another pair of legs passing him by. Whose they were and what they were like was immaterial. Tony was as indifferent to them as he now was to most things. He kept his gaze floorward and his thoughts somewhere in the neverland that was, by then, passing for his mind.

Fiona worked her way through the last remaining shops on her list and, on reaching the top of the High Street, turned right to complete the ellipse that would return her to her office. Once there she intended sending a very stern email, on the subject of vagrants, to George Wiley.

George was leader of the council and Fiona knew him personally. He and her father had been at school together, had read law together. She'd best copy her father in too, she'd thought, for good measure; urge him to have a word with George on the subject.

The problem with George, in Fiona's opinion, was that he was too, too, well, 'wishy-washy'. Yes, 'wishy-washy'; it was the only way she could describe him. He was a nice enough chap in general but definitely 'wishy-washy' when difficult decisions had to be made. Enough was enough though; this time George could jolly well do something about the situation.

A pity Daddy wasn't leading the council Fiona had mused; he'd soon have had things sorted. Her father was made of much sterner stuff than George. Unfortunately, Daddy was fully focused on his golf by then, particularly as the club had only recently made him chairman. He seemed to have little time for anything else.

Fiona would have also liked to have copied her mother in as

well, but her mother had never really taken to the internet revolution; getting her to use a mobile phone had been a big enough hurdle. A landline and an initialled, leather bound, paper diary to help keep track of her busy social calendar had sufficed all these years. Fiona's mother had seen no need to change.

Having reached the patisserie Albert stood looking into the window at the cakes and pastries, all waving at him, beckoning him to enter and sample them. He couldn't shake the thought of that young man though; it had troubled him the rest of his walk. This sort of thing shouldn't be happening, not in such an affluent city and certainly not at Christmas time Albert had thought. Not at any time in fact.

As he stood, rooted, Albert saw a reflection appear in the window, next to his own. It was Doris. He looked at her, quizzically. She smiled at him and nodded. He sighed and nodded in return.

"I'd better, hadn't I?" Albert said to her.

"Yes," he heard her say, "you'll only be unhappy if you don't, and you won't enjoy the tea. You won't enjoy Christmas either. It'll be bad enough for you without me there; having that young man on your conscience will only make it the worse."

Albert grimaced and entered the patisserie, but rather than going into the café proper and taking a table he joined the queue at the take-away counter to one side. When his turn came to be served, he pointed to a slice of cake he'd like; he'd already selected it whilst waiting. The young girl put it in a small box for him.

He paid with money from his trouser pocket and took charge of his possession, carrying it almost reverentially, as if he was carrying the Holy Grail itself. With a last and somewhat wistful glance back at the tables Albert headed out, back into the gloom.

By the time Albert was leaving the patisserie, Fiona had reached her office. Her resolve on the subject of vagrancy had hardened. Things had gone too far; this time George would have to take some action. He needed to lead the council on this; be firm. It was outrageous that decent people, by which she meant people like her, couldn't walk on the streets without feeling intimidated, though how a man, sitting in a doorway on a busy street was intimidating she never did explain, not even to George.

For their part, the Council were doing all they could to help alleviate the situation; at least as far as they were concerned, they were. After all, weren't they offering all the homeless the opportunity to return home by giving them one-way tickets back to wherever they'd come from? What more could they be expected to do.

Ironically, Tony was a local boy, born and grown in the area. Giving him a one-way ticket would only have served to return him to his present doorway.

On reaching Tony, Albert had paused and looked at the figure in front of him for just that moment. His stopping caused Tony to raise his gaze for once although he struggled to make eye contact. He wasn't sure what was happening. People rarely stopped but rather hurried on passed, ignoring him. The only people who did occasionally stop were the charity workers; the old man in front of him didn't look like one of those.

Albert reached into his waistcoat pocket and bent over towards the prone figure, putting the note firmly in Tony's grasp. Only when he was sure that the boy, as Albert thought of him, had the money safely in his hand did he let go and stand upright once more.

"There, son," said Albert softly, "you need it more than me," adding, "Merry Christmas," with a wan smile though he had to wonder what sort of a Christmas it was going to be for the lad. There wasn't likely to be that much cheer.

Tony didn't know what to say except a mumbled, "Thank you." He wasn't being rude or ungrateful, it was simply that, after so long, he'd forgotten many of the protocols of communication.

Having sent her email to George, the 'send' button having been thumped very firmly to ensure it went, Fiona had settled back into her chair, snug and smug, with little further thought for anyone but herself and immediate family. Shopping and the sending of the email had helped smooth her furrows.

Reaching for her 'to-do' list Fiona crossed out the actions successfully completed that afternoon whilst adding a few more she'd just thought of, to the bottom. Christmas was going to be wonderful, she thought. Even Radcliffe seemed to have been forgiven his ineptitudes for the moment.

Albert trudged back up the hill with his prize firmly in his grasp; he'd no intention of dropping it. "There but for the grace of God," he thought and sighed. "At least I've a home to go back to, even if it is empty."

"And a piece of cake," said Doris's voice in his head.

"And a piece of cake," he muttered to himself, looking down on his box. "Poor, bugger. Poor, poor bugger. He doesn't even have a piece of cake."

Any feelings of a burgeoning euphoria that Albert might have had, started to disappear faster than his pension seemed to each month. The melancholia that had been haunting him since Doris's passing made a vengeful return only, this time, it was rather because of Tony's plight, sitting there on that cold, unfriendly street, than for his own predicament.

Tony continued to sit where he'd sat all afternoon; after all, he'd nowhere else to go. He still clutched the money the old gentleman had given him. He wasn't sure what else to do with it. A tear welled in his eye; it had been a long time since he could remember such a kindness.

Homeless

by Glenda Bartlett

You might think that being homeless is living on the streets but you can also be homeless with a roof over your head.

It's sleeping in the car or in someone's poky box room alongside dusty boxes, discarded furniture and the owner's great aunt Mabel's stuffed stoat with eyes that follow you wherever you move and has an aroma that seeps under the duvet.

It's being in one room in a bed and breakfast with screaming and shouting and things bouncing off the walls in the next room.

It's once again travelling with your mum on a coach to your gran's cos your dad has gone off on another wild goose chase for a job he thinks he might like. And seeing the disappointment on gran's face and the shame on mum's when she opens the door.

It's renting one upstairs room for the three of us with a single bed from the sharp-faced woman. She turns the electric off at six in the evening, turns the water off at eight in the morning and checks before letting you in the door to make sure you are not bringing food in. I still chuckle wondering how long it took her to find the dead fish I left at the back of the wardrobe after we left.

There is no home, well not the sort in story books. Although we did have a home once in the middle of all this moving chaos. I had never seen my mum so happy. My uncle and aunt, and mum's sister visited and brought a tea-set. My mum made sandwiches and a cake and brought out her linen tablecloth, goodness knows how she had managed to keep hold of it. It had been a wedding present and she had embroidered it with exquisite flowers and foliage. It looked beautiful when it was spread over the card table as did my mum at that snapshot moment that my uncle captured. I treasure that photograph of mum and her sister, sitting at the table with my mum proudly pouring tea from the teapot.

I made a proper friend at last. Emily lived next door and we walked to school together and spent every moment we were allowed playing outside. Of course, it didn't last. Once again I was dragged out of my bed in the middle of one night and we were on the move again.

It's not much fun being the new girl at school and I was the new girl eleven times by the time I was fifteen. If you want to know what that's like then I'll tell you.

I was noticed as soon as I entered the playground, I'm sure there was a neon sign over my head flashing, 'NEW GIRL'. The other kids watched as I floundered like a fish out of water just inside the school gates. I didn't know the rules of this playground, they were different at every school. Who to watch out for and what were the dangers? My eyes would scan the kids looking for the odd ones out who might be a possible temporary friend and ally. What was the 'in' thing here? Where would I go when the bell rings? Did we have to line up in classes? I didn't know mine, or were we to line up as all girls and all boys? Every school was different, a minefield. The bell would ring and the kids would charge through the double doors. The anticipation and anxiety cemented my feet to a stop in the middle of the playground.

Don't get me wrong, I loved school, that's why I always insisted on going. Wherever we found shelter mum would find the local school. I loved the safeness of it, it was always there wherever there was. I loved to learn and I loved the routine of it. I didn't like the punishments for not having the correct uniform, why punish the kid? I had no means of getting a uniform. Punishments for not doing homework, punishments for not having cooking ingredients, they had no idea.

I don't want you to think my young life was all grim, a lot of it was but what I learned to survive at school made me the woman I am today. Schools had libraries, books were my ultimate lifesaver. My mum was an avid reader and I wanted so badly to dip into the books that she loved so I taught myself to read at the age of four. As young as I was instinctively reading was my escape. I read everything I could get my hands on. I stole books from libraries, comics from shops, and those stories took me away to another world. I escaped to be someone else. I developed a vivid imagination. When I started a new school, I would make up stories and adventures about my life. Instead of a misfit, I was interesting. I became the class comedian, the kid that with a funny comment or impersonation of a teacher could have others in fits of laughter. I discovered that I could write stories too. I don't have them anymore, when you constantly move you travel light.

I left my last school at fifteen, I couldn't face another one. The authorities didn't bother to find me. I wanted to work and earn my own money so that I could live on my own, in one place. I knew that I could always go back and study later if I wanted.

Being homeless wasn't my fault, I was a kid. Now as an adult, I am in a good place. I can't forget my childhood but I can live with it. I've worked in schools and sadly, I can see myself in other kids who supposedly have a roof over their heads but like me they don't have a safe home. When I talk to these amazing young people I joke with them, I read them stories. I snatch them out of lessons when I see they are struggling. I find their hidden talents, I hear their hopes and dreams for the future. I can tell them, 'I was like you once but as hard as this is now, it's temporary, you can go on, you will have a better life.'

I want to ask you, if you see a child at the school gates, scruffy, probably messing about, don't assume they're trouble, show them compassion. They might not have a warm loving home like your child.

Homeless Hope

by Sarah Luddington
Gay Romantic Fiction

The street light played on his face, distorting his features.

"Got any change?" he asked in a soft voice, hardly audible. He held out a grubby thin hand.

"I've seen you here before, right?" I asked, knowing full well I had but wanting to engage him in conversation.

He glanced up at me for the first time. His eyes were pale grey. I'd never seen anything quite like them. "You want me to move on?" he asked, the voice dull, uninterested and used to being victimised.

I crouched before him. "No, I don't want you to move on, unless you want to move on."

His eyes narrowed and became wary. "What do you want then?" he asked.

"Your help," I said honestly.

He frowned. "I don't fuck for less than a hundred." The distant, disinterested tone returned.

"I don't want to fuck you," I said. "I'd like to feed you, but I don't want to fuck you."

"I don't do blow jobs."

"I thought I said no sex," I repeated.

"I don't understand, if you don't want to fuck why are you talking to me?" he asked. I watched him take in the expensive boots, jeans, shirt and thick leather jacket.

"Maybe I just want to feed you," I said.

"Maybe you just want to eat my liver with a nice Chianti," he shot back.

I laughed and he managed a smile. "I've seen you drink, you

think I want your liver for anything including medical science?"

That raised a small chuckle. He looked at me again, assessing my potential for violence. "Just food?" he asked.

"Food, shower – alone – and a clean bed – alone – if you want one," I said.

"No strings."

"I do need your help with something."

"What?"

"Come and see, if you don't like the idea then you can still have the food and shower and bed but you can leave in the morning, no questions," I said.

He stared over my shoulder, then up and down the street. He fingered the filthy sleeping bag he sat in on the coldest night of the autumn so far and he made a decision. "I guess if you kill me I can haunt you forever," he muttered.

"An optimist, I like that," I said, standing up and giving him space to move on his own.

He rose slowly, his joints behaving like an old man's. As he struggled to gather his sleeping bag and push it into a torn rucksack I found myself watching the way he moved.

Long slim limbs, tall, broad through the shoulders. Dark blond under the dirt. High cheekbones, almost feminine features with full lips.

When he'd lifted the bag to his shoulder I made sure I remained out of arm's reach. He wouldn't welcome casual contact; those pale eyes were worn to stone through worry and hardship.

"This way," I said, cocking my head to the right.

He grunted and followed me across the busy London road. I stopped in front of my building's door and pushed in the code. The night porter would be asleep and I didn't want to wake him. The door opened silently and the young man looked over his shoulder at his previous address.

"You been watching me?" he asked before crossing the threshold.

"I noticed you but I haven't been watching you," I lied. "Do I need to invite you in officially?"

"I'm not a bloody vampire," he muttered.

I smiled to myself. Two literary references that could have come from a book or a film but it showed a spark of something inside him.

We walked through the large entrance toward the lifts at the back. Modern sleek lines of glass and steel surrounded us, broken only by large pieces of modern art in the abstract form. When we made it to the lift I pressed my thumb against the pad, a laser lit the screen for a second and the lift door opened.

"Fancy," my companion said.

"Expensive," I agreed.

"Looks like you can afford it," he said.

I shrugged and walked into the lift. He hesitated. It wasn't a large space he'd have to come close to me. I pushed my hands into my pockets. He stepped over the threshold and the doors closed. There were no buttons on the lift walls, my thumb print taking me to my apartment. We travelled up twenty floors and the doors opened, the young man left instantly.

I followed slowly. The doors opened directly into my private foyer. He stood and looked around, taking in the art, the marble, the fine furniture and large windows showing a good view over the river.

"Very expensive," he muttered.

"Drink?" I asked, moving past him slowly, giving him a wide berth. I didn't watch if he followed I just left the foyer and headed into my lounge. Books and art lined the walls, no TV in evidence. More pale marble and a single dark rug spread on the floor surrounded by cream leather sofas and chairs. The drinks cabinet was an antique as was my writing desk pushed up against the glass so I could stare out over the city seeking inspiration.

I poured myself a good shot of vodka and one for the young man. "Ice?" I asked, holding up the clear liquid.

"Sure, why not, I don't think it'll break your bank."

"No, probably not."

I walked toward him with the glass held out. He took it off me and downed the heady drink in one.

"So what are you? A banker?" he asked.

"No, I'm an artist and writer," I said.

"Famous?"

"In some circles."

"Not in mine?"

"No."

"Oh."

"What's your name?" I asked him.

"What's yours?" he asked me, a hint of challenge.

"Ben," I said truthfully.

"Kieran," he said in return.

"That's a good name," I said.

He shrugged and finally dropped his bag onto my clean floor. Maddy would have a heart attack when she came to clean.

"What is it you want?" he asked me, holding out his glass.

I refilled it. "Come on, I'll show you," I said. I returned his glass to him and led him from the lounge through a door opposite the one we'd already used. A short hallway and we hit the kitchen, sleek and very clean, another hallway and we reached my studio. A lot of glass filled the walls and ceiling. The views were spectacular and he paused to take it all in. I watched his eyes widen, the sudden innocence in them wonderful. He glanced at me and smiled in genuine warmth for a moment.

"It's beautiful," he said.

"Yes, I'm glad you like it."

"Who wouldn't?" he asked, walking toward the glass and peering down. "You can see my doorway."

"Yes," I said.

"You were watching me," he accused but he didn't seem wary now, just amused.

"Sort of. Here is why I need your help," I said, to distract him.

I walked to the centre of the room and pulled on a cloth covering my favourite easel. The cloth came away and vast canvas appeared.

"Wow," Kieran said.

"Hmm," I said.

"You're good."

"I have my moments," I said.

"No, Ben, it's amazing."

He walked toward the canvas with his hands behind his back and began to examine the figures in detail. A woman stood in a woodland, ethereal and distant. The figure of a young man stood, half sketched in the corner, that part of the canvas blank. I'd spent a long time on the texture and colours of the woman and woodland. My female model a rare beauty of the old style.

"I need a model," I said, pointing to the blank part of the canvas. "I can usually paint men without any trouble but this one..." I frowned, deeply troubled by my lack of recent skill. "This one I can't find. I can't see him," I said, tapping my head. "Then I noticed you as I was staring out of the window. You are the man. You are perfect." I looked at him.

"You want me to model?" he asked.

"Yes, it will be naked, I'm sorry but it has to be. We won't do that until you're comfortable of course and I'll pay you the usual daily rate."

"No funny business?"

"Not unless you count standing still for hours so an artist can paint your form in perfect, monotonous detail."

"I can stay here while you do this?" he asked.

"I have a room my models use. I keep strange hours."

He looked at the painting in detail once more, keeping his hands well out of the way. He then walked around and examined others. "They are beautiful. The figures, the scenes," he said eventually.

"Thank you," I said.

"You gay?" he asked.

I laughed. "Does it matter?"

"No."

"Good," I said without answering the question.

"You were going to feed me," he said.

"I was," I agreed.

I covered the painting carefully and left the room, Kieran coming with me. He kept stopping to touch the fabrics surrounding us and a soft, private smile played on his lips. I briefly wondered if I'd wake up and find the place stripped of valuables but I realised I didn't care. I just wanted to watch this young man move and listen to that soft voice.

We walked to the kitchen and I began to forage in the fridge.

"Do you have a beer?" he asked.

I picked one out of the cool box and handed it to him silently. The tick, fizz, swallow and sigh made me smile. Familiar male noises.

I cooked, pasta and sauce, he tried to eat nicely but the desperate hunger won out. I just watched him move, like a hungry predator. A young tiger who hasn't quite learned how to hunt alone yet and is suffering for his ignorance.

"You'll want that shower now," I said.

He pulled at his clothes. "I must stink." He sounded so miserable.

"I'll show you to your room, you can shower there. I'll find you some clean clothes, they won't fit you but they'll do. We can order more online or go shopping," I said.

"If something is too good to be true it usually is," he said.

I gave him a half smile. "Or perhaps you've paid your dues to Fate and she's sent you to me for a reward. Don't think too heavily about it, just have a little faith."

"I'm a bit short on faith," he admitted.

I didn't want to pursue why, I just wanted to allow him to be himself in my company. To be honest I wanted to continue to imagine his life, as I'd been doing for nights now, while I watched him in the doorway.

66

We walked to his room, adjacent to mine. I took the key out of the lock and handed it to him. "This is yours. I'll have you registered tomorrow at the front desk so you can come and go as you please."

He looked at the key. "Do you have one?"

"Somewhere but it's your room for now, not mine," I said.

He took the key and his fingers lingered for just a moment too long, he looked up at me, those grey eyes soft from the drink. "Thank you," he said.

I smiled. "You are welcome."

He went into his room and I heard happy noises coming from within. I turned away and returned to my room, finding a t-shirt, jumper and sweat pants that were a little too tight for me but should fit him closely enough.

He'd left his door open and I heard him singing in the shower, so I placed the clothes on the bed and retreated. It was two in the morning and I decided to retire.

"I think I'm going cross-eyed staring at that wall," Kieran said.

"Just a bit longer," I told him. I added one or two strokes with the fine brush I'd been using all morning on the large canvas. We'd been working together for a week, hour after hour, of sketches, rough paintings, gradually drawing him closer to the image I wanted for the final masterpiece.

With clean, cut hair just touching his shoulders and natural bright blond highlights among the dark blond curls, along with the clean shaved skin and less hunger biting his bones, Kieran looked like a Greek god come to life. A cliché perhaps, but so fucking true. He was beautiful. Perfect. And I was captivated by him. Every smile, laugh, bright glance or dark mood to sweep through his volatile mind entranced me.

I still didn't know why he was on the streets or where he'd come from originally and it didn't matter. I'd hardly left the apartment for days, just wanting to work in a fever before I lost my muse.

"There," I said. "You can relax."

He puffed out and instantly sat on the floor in a heap. "It's hard work this standing still," he complained.

"You do it so well," I said, adding just a little more to one aspect of his shoulder.

"We can do naked tomorrow if you want," he suddenly announced.

My paintbrush shuddered and I screwed up the stroke. I hardly noticed. I forced myself to remain calm, I didn't want to scare him off.

"That would be good," I said. "But only if you are completely comfortable."

He rose in fluid grace off the ground and approached me. I wanted to run. I stared into his eyes, knowing I was about to be devoured.

"I'm gay," he said. "I just didn't want you to take advantage. I've had enough of that in my life. I can't deal with it anymore."

"Kieran..."

"I know you want me, Ben. I'm ready. I trust you. No one has touched me for three years and four months." He picked up my hand, removed the brush, and placed it on his naked chest. I felt his heart pounding hard under my hand. "Make love to me, Ben."

"I can't lose you," I whispered. "If it means I don't get to touch you, that's alright, because I can't lose you."

"I'm not Dorian Grey," he said, smiling at me. "I'm not going to turn into some hideous creature on that canvas and imagine how much more of me you will come to understand to put into this painting and all the other's we'll do together afterwards. Ben, I want you to love me. Please. No one has ever been this kind to me, or looked at me the way you do. Please don't make me into something trapped in aspic forever."

I moved with a speed that shocked him. I grabbed his face hard and kissed his lips. His mouth opened and my tongue jousted with his, I groaned. We kissed for a long time.

Kieran finally came up for air. "Bed?" he asked.

"Mine," I said.

"Take off your shirt first," he said.

I frowned. "Why?"

"Because I know you are hiding something and I want to see it in the light of this room. The room in which I learned to love again," he said gently, touching my face.

I stepped back from him, turned and pulled at the shirt and jumper I wore in one savage movement. Cloth tore and I threw it on the ground as I turned back toward my would be lover.

"Oh, Ben," he whispered. "What happened?"

"Some scars are on the inside, some on the outside. A fire at the family home. That's where all the money came from. I inherited a title and lands. I was fourteen."

He came toward me and reached out a hand to feel the ridges and dips. The rough and the smooth. The deep wound that covered the right side of my body, arm and leg.

"It must have been terrible," he said.

"It was."

He looked up at me. "You are beautiful," he said, touching the scars trickling down the right side of my face. "Utterly beautiful, Ben."

I tried to smile but couldn't, his words difficult to hear. I was not beautiful.

He leaned into me. "You are beautiful and I am going to prove it to you every day we are together."

We kissed again, more gently and he led me from the studio to my bedroom. Could a god love a monster? I hoped so...

Samphire

by Michael Forester

When they said we smelled of Samphire and ocean salt their intent was kindness. In truth the odour that clung to us was nothing more than that of obnoxious bodily fluids and the twisted dreams of old men hobbling towards the grave.

We had, all three of us, arrived at the shelter within hours of each other on 19th December 2014. Though we shared nothing more than a moment, to those that looked on it was sufficient synchronicity at that pre-festive moment, to christen us 'The Three Kings'. Once this seasonal nomination had been universally adopted my two unintended associates were henceforth known as Gold and Frankincense and I as Myrrh. There could be no more fitting a name for me.

Though our cotemporaneous arrival was nothing more than coincidence, the fact that it took place on 19th December was not. We had each in our time stayed at St Solomon's Shelter for the Homeless before. Each of us knew that its policy of moving residents on within three days was relaxed during the week before and the week after Christmas. And though it was profoundly disagreeable to be ejected from our beds on New Year's Day to face a city like as not frozen to several degrees below zero, we all considered this a small price to pay for the luxury of two weeks punctuated by hot showers, and characterised by prolific warmth and sufficiency of food.

We were to receive an improbable visit from Santa Claus that year. It was due entirely to the strict 'no alcohol' policy maintained by St Solomon's. Signs as to the inviolable nature of this rule and the terminal consequences of its breech were posted at frequent intervals around the hostel. They were also explained to each man upon admittance. Why anyone would squander thoughtlessly the benefits we valued so highly on momentary stupefaction escapes my reason, for detection was inevitable and ejection from the shelter just as certain. But there again I am not an alcoholic. As it was, at 10.00 am on December 23rd, Frankincense grudgingly vacated the bed next to mine, packed his bag and left, a volley of incoherent but nevertheless incendiary expletives trailing out behind him until the closing of the door severed it. His bed remained vacant for a little under half an hour according to the plastic clock on the pine boarded wall of the dormitory.

The man shown to the vacant bed by the staff worker was a similar age to most of us who entered the shelter, that is, wholly indeterminate. He could have been anywhere between twenty-five and seventy-five. His skin behind the grime was olive coloured as far as I could tell, suggesting a Mediterranean origin. His beard was a greyish white, at least a month old, his hair unkempt and his face ingrained with the encrusted dirt of too many days on the road. In other words, he looked much as all of us did upon admission. What distinguished him was not his initial appearance but his voice. For there emanated from his barely parted lips an incessant stream of mumbles in a language clearly foreign, but which I could not easily identify. As it happens, I am fluent in German and Spanish, and speak passable Pashto and a little Dari. Something in his speech was familiar in the context of those latter languages, but if it was Arabic I could not yet pinpoint which dialect. His posture was bent and his gait shuffling. Somewhere along his journey he had encountered some seasonally mirthful individual who had provided him with clothing in the form of a Santa Claus suit, now, of course, dirty, torn and stained. Nevertheless, it was all he possessed and he continued to cling to it despite the protestations of the shelter workers. Presumably he did not understand its cultural significance. Finally, a compromise was reached despite the language barrier, whereby it was understood and agreed that while he bathed, his garments would be washed and dried, then returned to him. To no one's surprise he was immediately christened Santa.

A little before noon Santa re-emerged from the shower room, not exactly fragrant – that would typically take two or three more extended periods under the hot shower. However, he had at least shed the odour that the shelter workers euphemistically referred to as samphire. He returned to his bed and sat down, eying suspiciously all those of us who chose to be in the dormitory at that moment. From his arrival onwards Santa displayed the erratic behaviour of the deeply disturbed.

Inevitably most of those who sojourn at the St Solomon's shelter or others like it, are the walking wounded of a dissociated society that would mostly prefer to behave as if they did not exist. If you want to be generous at Christmas most people find it easier to send a donation to the Daily Telegraph annual appeal, or better still to Battersea Dogs home. Such gifts afford the donor the opportunity of a cosy feeling of generosity, a reassuring confidence that however much they spend on themselves or the over-privileged circle of well-stuffed family and friends around them, they did not fail to remember the 'less fortunate' at Christmas. The newspaper cutting, or the iPhone credit card number, or the appealing picture of a cute puppy retorts nothing in response that might disturb the warm glow of self-satisfaction that is, for most of you, an essential part of the festive season. But God forbid that you should ever make it through the doors of St. Solomon's or any of a hundred shelters like it up and down the land either as a helper or, like me, the personified excrement of a myopic self-absorbed uber-class. If you did, the reality of what 'life' means to the majority of the world's population would sink a dagger between your eyes and insert into the open wound enough metaphoric salt as to have you rubbing the incision for the rest of your life. You think I go too far in disturbing your self-satisfied indolence? Then let me tell you about Christmas in Helmand outside the military cordon, Christmas on the streets of Baghdad or —.

But then again, this is not my story I'm telling you, it's Santa's. Mine can wait a little while yet.

So he returned from his shower, and sat naked on his bed until the Santa suit was returned to him, clean, if no less torn than it had been when it was taken from him. He remained there in Buddha-like entranced immobility when it was offered back to him, gazing up into the eyes of the young centre worker who was holding it out with, I would guess, genuine warmth in his smile.

"Thank you," Santa finally said in the first words of English I had heard him speak. They were heavily accented words, words that carried an air of surprise if not suspicion, almost as if he were implying there had to be a catch to such an act of selfless generosity. But the young man continued to smile his honest smile and gestured that Santa should take the clothes. Finally, he opened his arms literally if not metaphorically and took the ragged suit back, whereupon he continued to sit unmoving, the garments draped across his lap as the come-and-go bustle of the dormitory continued around him. At suppertime we all moved into the dining room, leaving Santa behind us, still unmoving. When I finished supper I wanted to bring with me a plate of pasta for Santa. Such transport of food beyond doorway of the dining room contravened the rules of the hostel. I was not about to see myself follow Frankincense into the frozen world outside, so I explained the situation to a senior hostel worker who approved my intended act. Accordingly, I carried back to the dormitory a plate of spaghetti in tomato sauce and a spoon, a fork and a knife, figuring he would prefer to cut it up rather than try to wind it into consumable sized pieces. But when I got back to my bed he was asleep, his red trousers on in normal fashion and his oversize jacket covering his shoulders like a blanket. I left the food and the cutlery on the bedside cabinet for when he awoke and joined the others in the lounge for the evening's TV. On my return just before lights out he was still sleeping, though fitfully, and his vellicated movements had tossed his red jacket onto the floor, leaving his torso naked to the cold of the night. He was sleeping face down. I readied myself for bed and for sleep.

I cannot say what time I woke – I do not own a watch. The one I possessed in my former life was stolen from me during my first week on the streets and I knew if I acquired a replacement it too would disappear in similar fashion. I learned quickly that chronology has little significance to me and those like me. We are they who exist outside of time, whose 'before' and 'after,' whose 'yesterday' and 'tomorrow' are so similar to our 'now' as to confer an irrelevance upon time itself. You and those like you dream of inventing a machine to take you into the past or future. We are they who live our future today and will live our past tomorrow. You dream of inventing an elixir of youth, or an anti-aging cream that will preserve your life eternally. We have already discovered the true secret of everlasting life for the monotonous ache of eternity echoes incessantly through the empty caverns of our souls.

What woke me, though, was the fact that Santa's fitful, agitated sleep was now punctuated with a delirium of speech that, so far as I could tell, crossed the boundaries of language as easily as asylum seekers cross the boarders of continental Europe in pursuit of the Shangri-La beyond La Manche.

I propped myself up in bed on my left elbow facing him. Through the darkness I could see, but much more clearly hear, his torment. I reached out my hand, intending to rouse him from his terror filled nightmares, but hesitated momentarily. And as I did, he sat bolt upright in bed, his face contorted and his eyes wide open in the manner of men who have long since abandoned sanity. In his continuing sleep he grabbed me by the shoulders with a grip so tight I could not free myself. For a moment he seemed to struggle to find words, then said to me in a loud whisper in English, "My sleigh... knife... faster than bullet... I cannot forget... never forget... presents of the childrens. My sleigh… childrens. Presents of childrens… always with me." Then with no warning and without turning his face from me, his right hand released my left shoulder and reached to the bedside cabinet where his meal had long since gone cold. He picked up the knife and drew it slowly across his chest from his left shoulder to beneath his right breast. I recoiled rapidly, instinctively fearful that he would turn the knife on me in his frenzy. But he released it and it clattered onto the boarded floor as the shallow, fifty centimetre gash across his torso turned slowly red and oozed blood onto his legs where it seeped silently and invisibly into the red material. "My sleigh. Presents of childrens," he said calmly, "I never stop presents of childrens. Forgive. Padre. Forgive. God."

I took a decision at that point – an event so infrequent to one in my position as to be describable almost as a luxury. I could have roused the dormitory and called the duty officer. But if I had, Santa would have been ejected from the shelter at first light. Instead I lead him to the toilets at the end of the dormitory and staunched his bleeding with toilet paper while he watched me silently, his mournful eyes conveying everything he wished to communicate. The incision looked far worse than it was and clearly he, like me, had experienced worse wounds in too terrible a past to confront. Nevertheless, that past was seeping through the cracks of time and into the present once again in a manner all too familiar to us, the eternally damned.

Finally he allowed me to lead him back to bed where I settled him under his red jacket, for he still would not lie under the blankets and sheets. Amazingly all this had been accomplished without waking anyone else. As his breathing settled I returned to my own bed. As I lay in the darkness, too animated to sleep, I was at last able to turn my thoughts to his words and I reviewed what I knew:

An olive skinned man dressed in a Santa suit arrives at an English hostel for the homeless just before Christmas. Speaking of sleighs and children's presents he appears to believe he is

Santa Claus. And most uncanny in all of this he addresses me as Padre and asks for forgiveness of sins. It is over five years since I was last addressed as Padre.

I fell asleep turning these words over and over in my mind confused as to what manner of delirium could cause a man to believe he was Santa Claus. But in truth I was far more concerned about being addressed as Padre. For this was a term that belonged in the past I wanted to forget and it seemed that for me too, the past was seeping into the present and threatened to determine the future.

I awoke to the general bustle of a communal sleeping area rousing. Men moved about me, up and down the narrow corridor between our beds to the showers and WCs. Men retrieved shirts from hangers hooked over window latches to dry in contravention of the shelter's minor rules. Men retrieved toothpaste and brushes from secret compartments in their rucksacks. The values conferred on minor objects by those who possess almost nothing will seem strange to those who own everything they could want and more than they will ever need.

I turned to Santa's bed, but he was gone. Since he had left his red tunic I presumed he was showering and intended to return. When he did, the cut across his chest look sore but shallow. It was not bleeding. Santa smiled at me, though did not speak. Even to be acknowledged was, I thought, progress.

At 8.00 am by the dormitory clock we were ushered out and into the dining room. This time Santa came too, shuffling forward in the line like a natural. I went first and he took his lead from me. After breakfast we were free to do as we pleased. However, few chose to go out into the near freezing temperatures of a Christmas Eve morning. I sat in the lounge reading a two-year-old magazine while the television grumbled in the corner. Santa seemed content to sit by me silently. After lunch those that wished to sleep were permitted back into the dormitory. I exercised the option, as did two or three others not wishing to pass the opportunity of a soft bed, regardless of the time of day. Santa followed. As I lay down onto my bed he imitated me and was soon asleep. Then so was I.

I was woken by a violent shaking. I opened my eyes, still disorientated, to find Santa gripping my arm as the fire alarm went off. He was wide eyed and wild eyed with terror and yelled at me, "Padre! Padre! Incoming. Incoming," as he tried to drag me from where I lay and down into the narrow space between my bed and his.

As I shook sleep from my head I said, "No Santa. No incoming. It's the fire alarm test."

Then it was "Padre! Padre! Fire! Fire!"

Clearly I was to be granted no further sleep that Christmas Eve afternoon and for want of something better to do, decided to take Santa out for a walk. He seemed to understand readily and acquiesced with no resistance. As we left the hostel the festivities were in full swing about us with carols emanating from the shop doorways, chuggers' collection tins being rattled in everyone's faces, and later shoppers heaving parcels home barely in time for Christmas Day. At first Santa seemed to enjoy the level of activity we had stepped into and he eyed the activity as if he had never seen it before. This of course could not have been the case since he had come to the hostel only a little over twenty-four hours earlier and must have passed through similar waves of humanity to reach St Solomon's.

Inevitably we had not ventured far before fingers started pointing at his red suit. Santa did not seem to mind this at first. It was only when the children began to notice and crowd towards him his eyes filled with tears and he fell to his knees sobbing and rocking backwards and forwards. "Padre," he managed between sobs, "Padre. My sleigh... the childrens. Presents of the childrens. Always I have presents of the childrens." Then he turned his face to heaven and wailed so pitifully that all the little ones assembled backed away to their parents, uncertain as to how to respond to the unlikely sight of Santa Claus on his knees, weeping.

We were becoming a focal point and it would not be long before some voice of authority arrived to threaten us with action for disturbing the peace. I ushered Santa gently to his feet and led him, still weeping, back to the hostel. There I sat him on his bed, eased him gently back to the supine and waited until he drifted into an exhausted sleep. At bed time he was still sleeping.

Predictably, I was woken in the night. Again, I am unable to say at what time for certain, but I did not feel I had slept for long. This time, as he shook me from sleep it became quickly evident that this was no nightmare on his part. He was fully awake and seemingly, perhaps for the first time since we had met, in his right mind.

As he continued to shake my arm, he spoke to me rationally. It was a few moments before I realised he was speaking in Pashto.

كنت أتكلم الباشتو بادري ؟

"You speak Pashto, Padre? How is it you speak Pashto?" I can only assume that it had been my turn to talk in my sleep and it was this that had woken him. Was this the first time he had heard a familiar language so far from home? As I gradually came fully into the waking state, the conversation continued in Pashto, on his side fluently and on mine in a halting approximation. And on we talked, on through the night, through the barriers of language and culture, through the walls of fear and anger that we build to hide our self-loathing from one another.

I have thought back to that night many times, wondering what turn of coincidence or synchronicity had brought us together as Christmas day dawned over a sleeping city. Did we seek catharsis? Did we somehow permit ourselves the insouciant hope that the makeshift confessional we shared in the dark dormitory that night would somehow open the gates of the Celestial City on Christmas Day? For as it was, gates did open, but behind them lay not the gardens and fountains of joy with which we might once have populated our dreams of the future, but our own personal Belsens where the emaciated victims of our past crimes lay, stacked higher into the sky than a man's vision can penetrate.

His story and mine were not so dissimilar despite our backgrounds. I can blame no one but myself that following university I chose first to enter upon Catholic ordination and then, following the minimum ministerial experience period, the British army chaplaincy. I will not bore you with my years of field service prior to Helmand. Suffice to say that it was routine to the point of monotony. And it could easily have continued that way were it not for my confessional experiences of 2008–2009. When a man comes to you and confesses participation in the killing of innocents, do you grant him absolution? If his heart is repentant and the event unintended, you do, surely? When a second man enters behind the curtain and speaks of his torn conscience as one who has witnessed deliberate killings of civilians, how do you advise him? And when another and another and another follow them, speaking of the murder of non-combatants, do you condemn or do you absolve? Do you advise confidential conversations with commanding officers when you know their likely complicity in these acts? Do you recommend that distraught men who have participated in such acts by-pass the chain of command, knowing that the army will quite literally close ranks against such threats? Or do you, as I did, run out of platitudes with which to reassure others and yourself and eventually have nowhere to turn, not to God and not to man, and thus do the running out yourself. For that was what happened to me in Helmand. I ran out of resources, ran out of faith and ran out of the British Army.

And thus it was I found myself in another quasi-confessional that night, or at least in the presence of a man who needed desperately to confess his sins. Yet however anguish-laden my personal history, I could not have conceived of the unutterable pain suffered by the man before me, a fellow priest it transpired, in his case from the Nestorian Church in which he had cared for the souls of several Christian villages outside Mosul.

"Daesh came... June 2014," he started uncertainly. "The peoples... they had run from them from other villages. They told us Daesh kill. Daesh... rapio?"

"Rape," I corrected.

"Yes, rape. And kill like this." He drew his palm across his throat.

"Beheading," I ventured despite my distaste at the term.

"Yes, Daesh behead. Daesh rapio. Daesh kill. The men. The women. The childrens."

"Rape and behead children," I queried, "is that really what you mean?"

"Yes. Is so."

Thus, while the world looked on in astounded disbelief that such cruelties could be perpetrated in the name of a loving Allah, the army of darkness swept through village after village, destroying, pillaging, raping, murdering. Such was the way that news travels, the village in which Santa was teaching school in the church that day had but hours' notice of the approaching army and its nefarious deeds. Many parents came quickly, took their precious children and fled.

"Parents come," he continued. "Take childrens. Run. Daesh reach village. Still I have childrens, Padre. Six childrens. Small." At this point he gestured with his palm to indicate children of perhaps eight years of age or less. "Two boy. Four girl."

"I know Daesh is comings. Rapio childrens. Beheads. Burn bodies. Make watch."

He looked at me, huge sad tears rolling down his face, not knowing whether I would scream condemnation at him or take him in my arms.

"So I take childrens. One on one."

"One by one?" I ventured.

"Yes, one by one. Back of church. Behind..."

He was lost for the word in English.

"Behind the alter?' I questioned, my voice sticking in my throat.

He nodded. Then his words ceased and he gestured, representing his drawing a knife across each small throat, his right hand high above his left shoulder sweeping down across the child he held close to his heart for their last living moments upon the earth, just as he had done in his sleep the night before.

"I lay childrens here," he said, miming his laying each child before the cross of his Saviour and then waiting for the army of Satan. And as he waited in the darkness he felt, as he told me that Christmas morning, neither shame nor sorrow nor fear. All there was, was the church and the children and the alter and the blood. And he waited. And he waited. And he waited, for an end that never came.

"ISIS... not come to church. Like angel of death pass over Israel in Egypt. I wait. Wait. Wait. Wait. No ISIS. When I understand this, I leave church. I leave childrens in church. I look for parents. No find." His words came erratically through his tears. He wiped his hands perpetually over his face as if he could wipe away those tears and his words and his past in a single action.

During the following six months, if he is to be believed, Santa walked openly out of Syria and across Turkey, passing through Greece and Italy, boarding ferries and crossing frontiers without money and without being challenged. And all along his way he took food from shops and street vendors without being seen as if he were invisible to all, as if he had the mark of Cain upon him. Finally on that cold December morning he had arrived at St Solomon's in a Santa Claus suit with six months' encrusted dirt sticking to his body and a hardened layer of indifference clinging to his soul. And here, due to the ambiguities of the English language and his ignorance of English grammar, he spoke in his sleep of what I, his hearer, took as 'My Sleigh... childrens,' when a more fluent speaker

81

might have said 'I slayed children.' And when I understood him to say the 'presents of the childrens' were always with him, what he was seeking to convey was that 'the presence of the children was always with him,' for never, never could he forget the unforgivable sin he had perpetrated in the name of preventing an even grosser evil.

And so it was that before that dawn on Christmas morning, he asked me, "Padre, you forgive sin, please?" even though he knew I could not.

My inevitable answer, "Only God forgives sin, Santa," was met with the response, "Then you kill with knife. If you will not forgive Padre, please, you must kill." All this was said after the tears had ceased flowing. Now his face betrayed no more emotion than the stains of his earlier weeping. His own life meant nothing to him. All that remained for him was a hope that somehow the pain might be brought to an end.

Both I and the world had come full circle that Christmas morning. The world confronted yet again the slaughter of the innocents that purportedly had accompanied that first Christmas tide. And I personally faced yet again the request that I absolve the unabsolvable.

I did not grant him absolution. I did not kill him.

I never knew his name.

The Storyman

by David Luddington

Chapter One - The Man in the Square

The cardboard insulated me from the cold of the paving stones, but only just. The statue of Adam Smith towered behind me, cutting what warmth the fading sun still offered but at least offered some protection against the late afternoon wind. A little flurry of yellowing leaves scurried in a ball in front of me then continued on its way across the square.

The last of the tourists had disappeared at the hint of rain which had never materialised but then, they were always fickle here. Unlike its grander relatives of Trafalgar or Leicester Squares, Friedman Square held little of interest to casual tourism, no magnificent fountains or lions rampant, not even a gift shop. Just a functional, pedestrianised square with a scattering of statues honouring mainly obscure economists or second line politicians who never made it to Parliament Square.

The clock on St Matthew's Church moved its huge hand one click to six-twenty and I turned my head to the door of the Stanchester Building. The glass doors revolved and ejected their single passenger into the square.

The man in the suit paused and glanced up at the sky as he readied his umbrella in case it needed deploying. Deciding the skies offered no immediate threat, he pulled his jacket closer, dipped his head against the wind and headed in my direction.

As he did every day, he would stop in front of me, pull a handful of change from his pocket and drop it on my cardboard position. Neither of us would speak, we never did. Our communication always confined to small nods and slight smiles.

But today was going to be different. Today he would speak.

He scurried towards me and stopped, his hand already reaching into his pocket. His eyes widened slightly, his breath snatched and his body stiffened. He searched several pockets before looking directly at me. For the first time, I heard his voice.

"I'm sorry. I seem to have come out without any change. Tomorrow." He gave a forced, slightly embarrassed smile and continued on his way.

The next day, as usual he stopped in front of me again, this time with money already in his hand. "Sorry about yesterday," he said. "We had a leaving present whip-round for one of the office girls. It left me short. Here." he crouched and emptied the handful of change onto my cardboard.

"Choices come," I said.

"I'm sorry?" The man seemed puzzled.

"Yesterday, you made a choice and now today, both of our paths are different."

His eyes searched mine. "I don't understand."

"Tell me a story," I said.

"A story? I don't know any stories." He looked at his watch. "I have to go."

I watched him hurry across the square and disappear into the Underground entrance at the far end.

The following day, the tiny divergence of choice wiggled its butterfly wings and the paths widened.

The man in the suit emerged from his glass tower fifteen minutes early. He crouched in front of me as usual and dropped the change he'd been carrying.

"What did you mean yesterday? What story?"

"Your story," I said. "We all have a story and I would like to hear yours."

He shook his head slightly. "There's nothing to tell really. I'm a banker." He pointed at the big building. "I deal in currency. All very boring."

"Currency, the saffron of the modern world."

"I suppose. I'd never thought of it like that." He stretched a leg. Clearly, crouching was not something with which his body was familiar. "What do you... sorry... did, what did you used to do? You know, before..." His hand indicated my cardboard mat.

I smiled at him to ease his discomfort. "I trade in stories. So, in a way, we are the same. You and I."

"How does that work?" The man stood and eased his legs.

"I collect stories. I tell you some and you tell me yours."

The banker looked up at the church clock. "I have a train to catch. Maybe we can talk tomorrow?"

I nodded. "I have nowhere to be."

On Friday, the banker appeared even earlier. He hurried towards me crouched and dropped the change without a glance. "What makes you think I have a story to tell? I work in an office, it's all very boring." he said.

"Maybe you don't have your story yet. That's not important. You're a banker, we can work on credit. You can owe me."

"I will owe you a story?" His face dropped into a lopsided squint as he struggled with the concept.

"Yes, but like any transaction, there is interest to pay."

He twisted his legs until he was in a sitting position. "Interest?"

"Stories are the commodity of the soul. They have been traded long before man learned to make shiny coins and they will be traded long after the metal has returned to dust."

"Okay," he said. "I'd never thought of the similarities but what's with the interest?"

"I give you three stories and you return to me with yours, when it's ready." I fixed his eyes. "A three hundred percent interest rate." I smiled.

"What if I never have a story?" he asked.

"There is always a story," I said. "Choices come, new stories or old stories. The turn of a card, the spin of a coin. Sometimes chance presents new beginnings, the opportunity to start a new story. These are the stories I collect. Yours will come."

The banker's eyes stopped seeing as he churned the information. After a moment, he stood and said, "Monday?"

I nodded.

I watched as he crossed the square until the growing shade claimed him.

On Monday, the banker appeared even before the sun had shaded the far corner of the square. He dropped the coins and shuffled himself in a seated position alongside me.

"Okay," he said. "What happens now?"

"Now I tell you three stories."

Chapter Two - Terry's Story

The beach shimmered with hot, white flesh, broken only occasionally by the luminescent red glow of sunburned bellies and thonged buttocks. I stood at the top of the promenade steps which led down to the crowded sand, pausing a moment to let my nostrils acclimatise to the mingled delights of hot suntan lotion and cheap body spray.

I had steeled myself for this. I really had. Fully equipped with coolbox in one hand and paperback in the other, this beach was going to be the setting for my first holiday in eight years. Spanish beach, sangria, paella and peace. Karen had repeated that like a mantra in the weeks leading up to departure, clearly hoping to spark at least a glimmer of enthusiasm in me. And I had tried, really. But the sight which flopped out in front of me now more resembled one of Hieronymus Bosch's worst nightmares. A carpet of semi-seared bodies, laid end to end and cooking under a sun which gave no quarter for northern European flesh tones. Two weeks of enforced relaxation had seemed like a good idea but somewhere halfway up a mountain where telephones still only work by wire and social media is conducted via yodelling. Not at an all-you-can-drink Spanish Costa where fun is measured in decibels or by how far one can vomit.

Karen had meant it for the best, which is why I'd gone along with the idea. My work had torn my reason loose of late and doing something really stupid was beginning to feature high on my list of upcoming projects. Being a Special Effects Engineer might seem like a dream job for many, and indeed it was for me, at least it had been right up until the children arrived with their apps and showed the studio moguls how we didn't really need to *actually* blow up a bridge any more as it could now be done just by moving pixels around on a screen. The downside to being a Special Effects Engineer of course, is that when one starts to become terminally disenchanted, access to explosives is way too easy.

Karen had neatly intercepted a career defining moment by booking us a two week holiday in Bahia Blanca with the promise of a nice quiet beach and lots of lovely local food and drink to sample.

I stood for a moment longer, trying to calm the electric worms inside my head which demanded I scream then I turned and flip-flopped my way back along the promenade. A nearly empty bar with plenty of shade drew me like a millennial to an iPhone shop. I settled under a San Miguel umbrella and stretched my feet towards the sea. That was as close as I wanted to get. An attentive barman appeared and responded efficiently to my request for a gin and tonic. He even provided a small saucer of peanuts.

As the gin took hold, the electric worms calmed and the world became a safer place again. Of course, abandoning the scheduled sunbathing meant that I now had the best part of a day to fill. Karen and her mother had gone for a day of Spa Therapy so I was at a loose end. Always slightly dangerous. My working life consisted mostly of rushing against deadlines while trying to create an impossible effect for a manic director struggling to keep both his temper and budgets under control. Relaxation came infrequently and was usually as fragile as a cobweb in a gale.

A man sat at a nearby table, the only other occupant of the bar. His face wore a three-day beard which only accentuated a complexion which had clearly seen a lot more summers than I had. He caught my glance and his face resolved into a warm smile, his unnervingly cobalt blue eyes far too bright for his years. He nodded in greeting then stood to leave.

He dropped the paper he'd been holding on my table as he passed. "Choices come," was all he said then he was gone.

I reached across to pick it up. It was a local ex-pat newspaper with a garish headline about plans to start charging for parking in the local garden centre. Apart from the surfeit of adverts, the paper reminded me of the local papers of my youth where the biggest news items usually concerned lost dogs or somebody's retirement. I scanned the pages and settled on an article about ways to keep one's swimming pool clear of algae now the temperatures were rising. It wasn't the specific article which fascinated me, it was the fact that people actually had the time to worry about such things. Maybe one day.

Further into the paper, nestling within a banding of adverts for restaurants and English food shops, was a piece about a local amateur dramatics group looking for helpers for their Christmas production of Pirates of the Caribbean. The article talked about the joys of creating props from scavenging car boot sales. I could do that.

The gin spread its charm through my system and the warmth of the sun seeped into my tired soul. I put the paper down and slid a bit deeper into the chair, breathing in the soft breeze which licked across the Mediterranean. My eyes squinted against the brightness of the sea and on glancing away, they fell on the open newspaper to be drawn to an advertisement for a new development of luxury houses on the edge of the town. I skimmed the advert without picking up the paper. Overlooking a golf course, mountain and sea views. Discount. New build, no maintenance. Discount. Peace. Discount.

The barman brought me another gin and helpfully explained how to find Costa Properties. It was just a short walk, he assured me.

The short walk turned out to be a lengthy hike with coolbox and flip-flops only to find the estate agent's office was closed when I arrived. A hand written note in the window explained he was on a viewing and would be back soon. I decided to wait for a while and settled in a nearby bar with another gin and tonic. After half an hour, just as I was about to give up, a lanky youth wandered up to the door and let himself in.

I followed him in. "Hello," I said. "Any idea when they open?"

"We're open now," the youth said. "How can I help you?"

I wanted to ask if there were any grown-ups around but instead just pointed to the advert in the paper. "Do you know anything about this?"

"Oh, The Calle del Mar development. Very nice. Very exclusive. Would you like to see the plans?"

"Oh, it's not built yet then?" I was slightly relieved as it removed the niggle of curiosity but also, very slightly disappointed. "Never, mind. I was only curious."

"I'm Stuart, by the way." The youth held his hand across the desk and we shook. "Stuart Alinson."

"Terry," I said. "Terry England."

Stuart rummaged in a drawer under his desk and came out with a blue binder. "Here we go," he said. "Calle del Mar. There's only one unit left so you're lucky."

"Oh... I wasn't really..."

"Here's the artist's impression." He showed me a line drawing of a large house with palm trees in the front and mountains rising behind.

"When will it be finished?"

"Whenever you like," he said.

"I don't understand?"

"Oh, it's the system here. Builders don't finish the houses until somebody actually buys them. It means they can be finished to the new owner's specification. All very personal. Far better than buying a standard, boring box in the old fashioned British system."

"I see. I think. So, I can't actually see it until I've bought it?"

"Well, you can see where it is and you can see what they've built so far." He tapped at his computer. "You're in luck, I've just had a viewing cancel we can go now. Don't forget your coolbox." He stood and waited for me, then locked up and led me to his car.

We negotiated narrow streets designed for carts and dodged meandering pedestrians and suicidal cyclists.

"You planning to retire here? It's a lovely place, especially where we're going. Very peaceful and extremely low living costs." He didn't seem to expect an answer so I didn't offer.

The drive to Calle del Mar took me through a part of Bahia Blanca I'd not visited before. Wide, palm tree lined avenues neatly banded with the greenest grass I'd seen since leaving Somerset. And gates. There were lots of gates, mostly big and imposing, many with pillars topped by various creatures in carved marble.

We stopped alongside the shell of a house with metal props holding the ceilings up and haphazard scaffolding clinging tenuously to the walls.

"Here we are," said Stuart. "Plot twenty three. I was hoping José would be here." He pulled his phone out, stabbed some numbers then jabbered briefly to somebody I assumed was José. He finished the call and turned to me. "He'll be along shortly. He said he'd meet us in the bar."

We drove another five hundred metres and stopped outside a bar announcing itself as the Expats. We made our way into the garden area and ordered drinks. I stuck with the gin and tonic, it doesn't do to mix drinks at this part of the day. Last time I did that I ended up buying a sit-on lawn mower. To be fair, it was a bargain, it was just that my lawn was only twenty square metres and an electric shaver would have been more appropriate.

"You'll love it here. Two minutes to the beach, or if you want secluded, there's a small cove just to the east, about two kilometres. Always empty, even in August. Then up there." He pointed at the mountains behind us. "Up there you can walk for days and only see a couple of eagles or an ibex. Too quiet for me though." He turned towards the sound of approaching footsteps. "Ah, here he is, now."

José greeted me with a hug then sat down and pulled out a large notepad. "You like marble?"

"Um... yes?" it seemed like a rather random question.

"What colour marble you like?"

"Oh, just the usual, I suppose."

He made notes in his book.

"What's he doing?" I asked Stuart.

"Just taking notes about your preferences. Shall we go look at the house?" He stood without waiting for my answer.

I finished the gin and followed him to the car and back to the house. José pointed out various trip hazards as we negotiated incomplete floors and precarious staircases. For a shell, the building promised to be spectacular. It was a huge plot, and the rooms light and airy. Although, that may well have been down to the lack of walls. The mountains behind us raked into a sky so blue it made my eyes hurt. And to the front, the Mediterranean teased between the rooftops of the houses across the street with the blue divide between sky and sea almost imperceptible.

"The golf course is just there." Stuart pointed to a brown, levelled patch of earth about two hundred metres away. "And over there," pointing at a large hole with an ancient bulldozer next to it. "That's the community swimming pool."

We spent about half an hour looking at semi-plastered

brickwork and dangling wires before Stuart suggested we head back to the bar where we could chat in more comfort.

José chattered continuously on his phone during the short drive and continued as we found a table.

"So, are you retired?" Stuart asked after the drinks had arrived.

"Coming up for it, I think," I said. "I work in films, special effects."

"That must be exciting," he said.

"It used to be. But work is drying up now. The big studios need to tighten their profits and if they can get away with CGI rather than really having to blow up a building then they will."

"Well, this place will certainly let you enjoy your retirement," he said. "Clean air, low cost of living, great community. Do you sail?"

"What? No, I've never tried."

"I'll introduce you to the chairman at the yacht club. Lovely chap. Used to have a Ferrari dealership in Lambeth."

José finished his call with a slightly annoyed harrumph and stuffed the phone in his bag. He exchanged some rapid and thick Spanish with Stuart then they both looked to me. I wondered if my head had just gone as fuzzy on the outside as it was feeling on the inside.

"It's probably a long shot," Stuart ventured. "But José has just been offered a huge contract to build a house for Tiger Woods. You know, the golfer? He's really keen on this course. Anyway, José needs to free up a bit of capital to start work and he's prepared to take a loss on the house you're looking at so he can secure the contract. I told him he's crazy but you know what the Spanish are like. What do you think?"

"Um... well... I don't know... I wasn't really..."

"Would you like another gin?"

My breakfast coffee the next day only pushed at the edges of my hangover and I made it to the third cup before the fug finally started retreating. I looked up at Karen. Her look was uncomfortably familiar, the one which awaited the apology for sins I couldn't quite remember.

"Well?" she prompted.

I rubbed at my thumping head in an attempt to clear the mud. I remembered the beach. I hadn't made it to the beach. The man in the bar and the estate agent. Oh yes, the estate agent. Stuart. Pushy sort. And the contract. Ah, that wasn't good. I shouldn't be remembering a contract. I fumbled through my pockets and pulled out a wodge of paper. Important looking paper. Whoops.

I smiled weakly at Karen. "How do you feel about moving to Spain?"

Chapter Three - Michael's Story

I pulled my collar up against the cold and stamped my feet to keep the circulation going. I neared the front of the queue and the air was now rich with the smell of lentil soup. The sweetest smell in the world. You can keep your caviar and foie gras, when hunger digs deep and the wind cuts to your soul, there is no better smell than lentil soup. Sally's Kitchen consists of a loosely converted mobile library van with a serving window cut in its side. Of all the soup kitchens in London, Sally's Kitchen had always proved the most reliable and always turned up, whatever the weather.

I held out my mug and the woman behind the range smiled and ladled it full. I picked a bread roll from the box on the counter and found myself a seat on a pile of pallets.

"Hey, SAS," I heard a voice greet and looked up.

Big Jerry wandered over from the soup truck and nodded at me. "Move up."

I shuffled across the pallets to give room. "I keep telling you, I was only assigned to the SAS, not really one of them. Just their computer guy, sort of along for the ride."

"Yeah, yeah. You guys are all the same." He tapped the side of his nose with a woollen gloved finger. "Don't worry, your secret's safe with me." He sniffed at his mug. "What've we got?"

"Lentils," I said.

"It's always bloody lentils."

"I like lentils."

Big Jerry grunted and spooned the thick soup from his mug to a mouth which lay hidden somewhere behind a wild beard. When he'd scraped the last lentil out he said, "Where're you kipping these days?"

"You know, shelter to shelter. I'll try Hampdon Road tonight. They've usually got a spare place." I wiped my mug clean with a serviette and stuffed it in the side pocket of my Bergen.

"I've just moved in with a squat up Camden way. They're a bunch of nutters but there's plenty of space. I'll take you there if you like?"

The Camden squat was a large, rambling Victorian building spread over four floors. Boards covered the ground floor windows and access was only available via a hinged plank which gave the appearance of securing a side door.

We slipped through the gap and Jerry yelled, "Only me." Then he turned to me. "They're a bit paranoid. Anybody not wearing a tinfoil hat is CIA."

A voice called something from a back room but I couldn't make it out. We followed the sound of the voice and arrived in the shell of what had once no doubt been a luxurious kitchen. The room was clean enough but sparse. A naked bulb dangled from the ceiling illuminating the marbled work surfaces. Several butane gas stoves sat on the marble and the doorless cupboards were stacked with tins and packets of dried foods.

A man in an army jacket turned towards us. "Grab yourselves a cup, tea's up." His voice gave his roots as Newcastle but the DPM print of his jacket said Russian infantry.

I trusted the voice.

Jerry took a couple of china mugs from a shelf and handed one to me and the man poured tea into them. We sat at a massive but very battered pine table.

"My name's Sid," the man said.

"Michael," I said.

"Michael's ex SAS," said Jerry. "So don't mess with 'im or you'll get a karate chop."

"Assigned to SAS," I corrected. "Just the communications guy. Computers and stuff. And I don't know karate."

"We got a Marine upstairs," Sid said. "And a couple of other squaddies around. Has Jerry told you the rules?"

I shook my head.

"No hard drugs, no fighting and keep your own bit clean."

"Seems fair," I said.

"And if you bring the cops in, you're out. No discussion. Clear?"

"Crystal."

"Drink your tea and I'll show you where you can kip."

Sid led me to a dangerous looking staircase with more holes than treads and bits of rope as bannisters at the more tricky parts. On the first floor he took me into a room which was laid out with several tables and chairs. A hotch-potch of computer equipment filled every available flat surface. Ancient laptops, half built chassis and open towers mingled with various types of ancillary keyboards, modems and screens, mostly CRTs. A mountain of wires weaved their way through the scattered components.

"You'll like this." Sid waved his arm round the room. "It's our control room."

"Impressive," I said. "What's it for?"

He gave me a puzzled look. "Counter protection," he said as if I should have been obvious.

"Counter protection?"

"Yeah, they think they've got the drop on us, but we're

watching them. We know what's going on."

He led me up the next two flights of increasingly precarious staircase and indicated a large corner room. "You're in here, catch you later." He turned and picked his way back down the stairs.

The room was light and airy with unblocked windows, half of which still had glass. The walls showed patches of yellowed plaster where the daisy print wallpaper had peeled away. On the floor lay a couple of mattresses and several bedrolls. I found an empty corner, dumped my Bergen and unrolled my sleeping bag to stake my territory. To settle the nagging gremlins, I did a quick reccy of the house. What each room looked like, ways of possible escape or forced entry for undesirables. I knew it was silly, I knew I was just giving in to the gremlins but there was no point in resisting. They always won in the end.

Once satisfied that I understood the layout, I left the house and found a nearby pub for a nightcap. The Phoenix welcomed me with a real fire, comfortable seating and most importantly, a well-stocked bar. There was only one other occupant, a slim man with a face which looked hewn from ancient olive wood. He glanced up as I entered and eyes the colour of a desert sky at midday scanned me like a laser sight. His appearance was perfectly harmless but something about him set my senses on edge. He returned to his newspaper and I took a pint from the bar and sat with my back to the wall, facing the door. Old habits.

I pondered on the house. As Jerry had said, they seemed like a bunch of nutters but they were harmless nutters and they had a house. I could play nicely for a while. The pint hit the spot and the fire eased my bones. If the army had taught me one thing, it was to take my comforts where I could find them.

The man at the other table stood and my overactive paranoia twitched. He walked towards me and I planted my feet firm on the floor, hands loose.

He gave a smile as he passed my table. "Nice evening," he said and dropped his newspaper on my table. "Here, I've

96

finished with this. Choices come." He didn't expect or wait for a reply. A slip of cold air from the door and he was gone. I shivered as something touched my soul.

After a moment of self-admonition, I relaxed, slumped back in the chair and picked up the paper. It was a local weekly but not one I'd seen before. I thumbed past local news titbits, adverts for second-hand cars and massage parlours then a full page article caught my eye. Local MP Stephen Lethbridge had just been appointed Minister for Disability. I read through the article. He was busy catching votes by announcing a new clampdown on benefit levels, for working age people. He was going to save the government millions by clawing back housing allowances to single people. I remembered him from a few years ago. He'd been tangled up in the middle of the expenses fiasco when he'd claimed for a treehouse to be built for his daughter at his Berkshire estate. It had cost something ridiculous like a hundred-and-fifty grand. I folded his grinning face to the table and returned to my pint. Scum.

I made the beer last as long as I decently could then headed back to the squat. Several people were busy in the Control Room so I stopped to chat.

An ageless man in a fleecy checked shirt broke from his screen just long enough to stare at me and announce, "You're new."

"Just arrived," I said.

"How do we know you're not an avatar?" he asked. "You look like an avatar."

"How would any of us know?" I replied.

"I know," he said and returned to his screen. "I can see the phase shift. Dead giveaway."

A girl in a Metallica T-shirt and genuinely ripped jeans smiled at me. "Hi, you must be Michael. I'm Suzy. Do you know TOR?"

"Sure," I said. "Problem?"

"No, just need more hands. Here, have a go on this one."

She nodded to a bastardised computer rig next to her. "We've been trying for a DDoS attack on the CIA but we haven't got anywhere near enough bots yet."

"You're going to have problems there," I said. "Those guys aren't stupid."

"So they'd like us to think. But Jacko brought down one of their drones yesterday. It was taking pictures of us. Jacko sent it for a swim in the Thames." She laughed.

I thought it fairly unlikely and probably, they'd just splashed some kid's toy but what the hell.

Suzy's fingers fluttered over her jury-rigged machine as she spoke. "So, how come a guy with your skills ends up sleeping rough?" she asked.

"Oh, the army gave me a ticket home but I couldn't get work. Then the DWP screwed up my benefits and the bank took the last of my rent money in charges."

"Tough."

"There's others worse off, I've still got both legs." I sat at the computer, downloaded some software and sent it out looking for weak modems which could be recruited as bots for whatever project this lot had in mind. My idea of fun.

The following morning, I re-joined the Control Room crew. A guy with a green bobble hat and green woollen jumper greeted me.

"Hi, I'm Derek," he said. "You must be Michael. Suzy told me you're shit-hot with APDos. Cool."

"I got lucky," I said. "I was trained by the best."

"We're trying to get into Boscombe Down," said Derek. "But they've got a mother of a firewall."

"They would have. What the hell do you want to get in there for? It's only an RAF testing site."

"It's where they're holding the aliens. Everybody knows that."

"Ah, okay." I wasn't going to argue. I'd been through Boscombe Down a few times and I was fairly sure there were no aliens there. That was probably something I'd have remembered.

I spent the morning helping Derek through the MOD firewall. I should have felt guilty, but I didn't. They'd used me up then dumped me when I'd cracked under the pressure, so sod them. Sod them all, I owed them nothing.

I spent several days getting to know the people and generally having fun poking about in what were supposed to be the most secure sites in the world. The other occupants in the house were an interesting bunch, a real mix of computer nerds, new-age hippies and conspiracy theorists. Each had their own tale to tell and oddly, I began to feel very much at home. Even if most of them were even crazier than me.

One morning, I was scanning the Houses of Parliament website looking for weaknesses when I saw a picture of Stephen Lethbridge, Minister for Disability. His smiling face tore at the last few remaining strands of my reason and I wanted to destroy him. I needed to make him suffer. I wanted him to know what poverty felt like.

By lunchtime I'd scraped enough background information about him from Social Media and the House of Commons website to begin my attack. It took another three days for me to inject a Trojan onto his House of Commons computer. He'd been difficult but I was patient and he needed to be lucky every time, but me, I only needed to be lucky once.

Once I had remote access to his computer it was just a matter of waiting until he accessed his bank. Two days later, I had full access to all of his banking records and investment portfolio. I then shut down his own access while I went to work.

I'd never intended stealing his money, although at this point it would have been easy. But how would I hold on to that? It would be setting a beacon to Special Branch or MI5, shining like a supernova in the darkness. No, far better to make him suffer. Money in a bank is just ones and zeros. Turn all the ones into zeros and it all just goes away. No trace, no trail to my door.

No easy way of getting it back.

So that's exactly what I did.

I watched in quiet satisfaction as the numbers slipped away. A cascade of nothingness settling on every corner of every account he owned. Two hours later and the Right Honourable Stephen Lethbridge was bankrupt. He was so broke even Wonga would have turned him down. Furthermore, no crime had actually been committed. I hadn't stolen a thing. In fact, I was going to make him a gift. I returned to his account the sum of thirty-three pounds and fifty-five pence. The exact amount of disability payment due to a returning serviceman. For good measure, I attached a reference note, 'Your weekly payment'.

I closed the computer and pushed back in my seat.

Suzy looked over at me. "You alright?" she asked.

"I'm good," I said. "I think I might just stay here a while."

"That's cool," she said. "They're a good lot here, once you get to know them." She studied me for a moment then smiled and added, "And you look like you could use a new start."

Chapter Four - John's Story

I picked up my copy of The Stage from the newsstand on the way to the tube station. Sam always kept one by for me, although, I should really cancel it. I rarely read it these days. My act had remained neatly stacked in chests and boxes in my lockup for three years now and the likelihood of me raising it again retreated with each layer of dust it accumulated. Every time I even contemplated resurrecting it, thoughts of Amy took over any rationality and the idea of training a new assistant was just too horrible. And what use is a stage illusionist without a glamorous assistant?

The noise of a small but vocal crowd snagged my attention, they gathered around one corner of the tube entrance. That was unusual. I surveyed the area and noticed two men standing some way from the group. They looked outwards. Ah, they would be the scouts. I moved closer and heard the unmistakable patter of the Three Card Monty game in progress. I eased my way into the group. Several people pressed inwards towards the dealer. One man appeared to be winning consistently. He would be the shill. The Judas Goat.

I approached him. "You seem to be doing okay," I said.

"I've got a cheat," he said in a loud whisper. "I've folded a corner on the queen, see?" He nodded towards the cards. "I can win every time, the dealer's a mug."

Indeed, one of them had a bent corner. A common ploy to make the punter feel they were able to take advantage of the dealer.

I put my hand in my pocket and pulled out a bundle of notes. "I'm up for betting all this but I'd rather not have all these separate notes flying about. You've got some fifties there, can you change these for a couple of those?"

"Sure." I gave him a pile of tenners and took his two fifties. "You'd better check it," I said.

He counted the notes and looked up at me with a frown. "There's only nine," he said.

"Damn." I put my hands into my pockets, pretending to search. "Sorry, I haven't got any more. Here, you give me those back." I took the notes from his hand. "I'll give you six of these and another couple of twenties, that makes a hundred now. Do you have another couple of those?"

He nodded and drew two more fifties from his pocket. I watched his eyebrows knit in confusion so I increased the pressure by glancing furtively around as if on the lookout for police.

His eyes followed mine and he succumbed to the rising anxiety, handing me the notes.

"Perfect, all square now, thanks," I said and pushed my way past him to the makeshift table. I studied the dealer for two rounds. Nothing complicated. A simple palm, a quick pass and he turned over the queen exactly where I predicted. I watched another time just to be sure then put my four fifties on the table.

The dealer paused and locked eyes with me. It was a big bet and bound to cause thought. I winked at the shill, making sure the dealer saw the supposed conspiracy.

The dealer relaxed, covered my notes with four fifties of his own and started his patter. "Where she goes, nobody knows." He flicked the cards around the table. "Watch the lady, she's your ticket." I saw the switch and another card with a folded corner took the place of the original. He was very good, it was almost perfect.

The cards stopped moving and I pretended to hesitate for a moment before placing my forefinger on the card I knew in reality to be the queen.

The dealer's eyes narrowed. He looked up at me. "I like you," he said. "So I'm going to give you chance to change your mind."

"No thank you," I said. "I'm happy with this one."

The dealer glared at the Shill. Usually, if a punter ever selects the correct card, the Shill simply places a larger bet on the same card and the dealer claims to only ever take the larger bet. Only this time, I'd not only taken a chunk of the Shill's stake in my switch, but I'd also dipped his pocket for the rest.

The Shill gave the dealer a shrug to indicate he couldn't cover the bet. I knew the dealer would have a fall back so I watched as he reached forwards to turn the card and I noticed the shape of his hand change. A sure sign of a palm in progress. I beat him to the card and turned it over myself. A collective intake of drawn breath hissed around the group as the queen appeared.

"I've won," I called loudly with an exaggerated laugh. With the group now on my side, he wouldn't try to renege.

The group applauded and I gathered the cash. I took a mock bow then headed for the tube entrance, dropping my win in the tin of a homeless man who sat just outside the station.

I took the tube to Piccadilly Circus and walked the five minutes to Kev Blake's Magic Studio in Wardour Street. Kev's place covered the first floor of a remarkably forgettable Georgian building in a particularly boring part of an otherwise perfectly normal London street. He greeted me with a warm handshake and a gentle pat on the back.

"How are you doing, John?" he asked.

"So, so. A day at a time."

"You got something for me?"

"An interesting little effect I've been working on for a while now." I took a bottle from my bag and set it on his counter.

Kev picked it up and studied it. "Okay, it's a clear wine bottle. Looks genuine enough. What does it do?"

I pulled some glass marbles from a little bag and gave him one. He rolled it in his fingers then tapped it on the wood of the counter.

"And a marble," he said. "Go on, impress me."

I took the marble from him and placed it on the top of the bottle. It was, of course, too large to fit through the neck. "Watch," I said and pressed my finger gently on the marble. It dropped through the neck and tinkled to the bottom of the bottle.

Kev picked up the bottle and held it upside down. The marble stopped at the narrowing neck. He shook the bottle, listening to the sound of glass on glass. "That's impressive." He handed it back to me.

I upended the bottle and the marble dropped into my hand. "It's a variant of an effect created by David Nixon," I said.

"Do I get the exclusive rights?" Kev asked.

"If we strike the right deal." I smiled.

We haggled good naturedly for a few minutes and agreed on a royalty. Since leaving performing, I'd generated a reasonable income licencing some of my creations and Kev was one of the most respected magic dealers in the business.

"You should really go back to performing," he said. "It

would do you good."

"Maybe one day."

"Well, you need to do something or you're just going to eat yourself up."

I took the afternoon tube back and found a quiet carriage with only one other occupant. He looked to be a homeless type, an army coat and a weathered face with a deep tan, far too deep for a London climate. He glanced up from his newspaper and fixed me with eyes which had no right to be sitting in that face. They lit with a blue the colour of burning sulphur and with a clarity which clashed sharply with the man's age-worn appearance.

I found myself locked to his eyes for a moment then forced myself to look away for fear of seeming rude. I pulled out my copy of The Stage and looked blindly at the words on the paper.

The train slid to a halt and the doors hissed loudly. The man stood and walked past me on his way to the door. He dropped the newspaper he'd been reading on the seat next to me. "Here, I'm done with this. Choices come, chance presents change." he said and stepped onto the platform.

I twisted to watch the departing platform as the train swished into the tunnel but there was no sign of him. My eyes slid to the paper. It was a local freebie with which I was unfamiliar, mostly adverts but with just enough editorial to justify calling itself a newspaper. I thumbed through the pages in between glancing up at the station signs each time we stopped. My aimless scanning stopped at a corner advert for a séance being held in the old Tiffany Theatre. There was nothing unusual about the advert but it was the picture of the medium which caught my attention. He was billed as the Great Geoffrey, your personal contact with the other side.

After Amy, I'd spent time with a few mystics and mediums. I knew it was silly, I knew they weren't really talking to her. But I held hope. The Great Geoffrey claimed to be a Master of the

Hidden Temple and held the sacred scroll of Bastet which gave him mastery over the spirit guides. The only problem was, I knew the Great Geoffrey when he was Gilfrey the Mentalist. A second rate pub magician with a mind reading act which barely scraped past his average inebriated clientele in an East End pub. An act with a heavy reliance on his attractive wife secretly chatting up a few likely candidates in the bar and slipping him information for his great reveals during the act.

For a fifty-quid-a-night, pub-circuit entertainer, he was probably reasonable value to a landlord wanting to pull in a few extra punters on a quiet night. But now it looked like he'd graduated to another level. I folded the newspaper and stuffed it in my pocket then glanced up as a station sign appeared outside the window. Damn, I'd missed my stop.

The Tiffany Theatre lay forlorn and neglected in the once fashionable Shapwell Street. In its day, it had hosted some of the greats of the Music Hall and even as late as the nineties it still held esteem to touring shows. I'd even played there myself once. But now, it served as a hall-to-rent and mostly held home to local rock bands, wedding receptions or rave parties.

I hovered in the foyer bar amongst the arriving attendees and kept a watching eye for any faces I recognised. Most of the audience appeared to be elderly with the majority female, They gathered at tables and chatted animatedly, probably about other séances they'd attended as there seemed to be a lot of mutual recognition amongst them. It didn't take me long to spot the plant. It was no longer his wife, maybe she'd left him or perhaps time dictated he needed somebody younger and sassy. The girl was small and trim, dressed in jeans with a white, low cut tee-shirt which covered everything while still revealing that which was being covered. She chatted with various people before eventually latching on to one elderly man who seemed fascinated with her tee-shirt. They huddled into conversation for a while then she stood to leave, kissing her finger tips and planting them on the man's forehead. I watched as she slid into a corner and tapped furiously into her smartphone. As she finished and turned back towards the bar, I gently collided with her, spilling a little splash of beer on my shirt.

"Oh, dear. I'm sorry," she said.

"No problem. I wasn't really paying attention. I just need a…" I pointed towards a serviette holder on the bar and threaded my way through the people.

She followed, as I knew she would. "Here, let me." She took a serviette and dabbed at the wet patch. "You here for the séance?" she asked.

"Yes," I said. "I've never seen him but I've heard he's really good."

We chatted for a while. I bought her a drink and showed my infatuation with her charm. She gently probed and prodded, tweaking snippets of information from me a bit at a time. To give her credit, she was very good and had a natural style which was quite disarming.

Finally, she clearly had enough information from me and excused herself saying she'd just spotted an old friend. I watched her leave the bar, no doubt to organise her notes before moving on to somebody else.

The bell rang for the ten minute warning to the start of the show. I made my way up the once grand staircase, showed my ticket at the door and found my seat. The house darkened and a voice announced the commencement of the Event. The Great Geoffrey took the stage like the professional he clearly was and I couldn't deny him his presence.

"Ladies and Gentlemen," he started. "Seekers of the truth, believers and even sceptics, you are all welcome."

A trickle of applause spread round the room and he held his arms high. "I have somebody from the other side, we can begin." He settled himself at a large table which dominated the centre of the stage. A pair of silver candlesticks graced the table and their faint glow flickered shadows across his face. Behind the table, the rear of the stage was in complete darkness. I wondered what contraptions and devices hid within the shadows.

He slammed his hands on to the table top and the candles shimmied under the force. A nice touch, I thought. He threw his head back as if being controlled by unseen forces then called out, "Sheila? Do we have a Sheila? I have a visitor from the Realm who has a message for Sheila."

A woman stood up three rows behind me. "I'm Sheila," she called.

"My guide tells me she is communicating with Guy. Is that name important to you?"

The woman's voice trembled with fear. "Yes, that's my son."

"Please come closer, Sheila. He wishes to give you a message."

An assistant led the woman to the stage where she stood next to the table.

The Great Geoffrey spoke in some form of gibberish then turned to the woman, his face tinged blue and an ethereal glow took his eyes. It was all very impressive, as the collective oohs and aahs of the room testified. For me, I scanned the wings of the stage until I found the discreet but tell-tale glow of the blacklight source which was perfectly focussed on the performer's face. Nicely done though, I'd give him that.

"Guy wants you to know that he's happy and no longer in pain. Does that mean anything to you?"

The woman nodded and tried to speak but the words wouldn't come.

"He says he knows you did everything you could but it was his time." He reached a hand up and with a little gesture, he snatched a feather from the empty air. A neat little twist on the appearing card effect.

As one, the audience gave a start followed by a nervous laugh. He waved his hand gently and the feather drifted through the air and hovered in front of the terrified woman.

107

"Take it," he said. "It's a gift. A feather from his angel wings."

My desire to leap out of my seat and drag this man to the floor filled my being and I dug my hands into the seat rests to control the impulse. It gradually subsided to a manageable level. The woman took the feather and made her way back to her seat.

Another two victims followed and we were witness to more feathers, a levitating candlestick and even a ghostly mist at one point.

And then it was my turn.

"Peter Venkman," the Great Geoffrey called. "I have a contact from the other side for Peter Venkman. Is he here?"

I stood. "Yes, I am Peter Venkman." This was the risky bit. Would he recognise me? My real name of John Barker would have been an immediate giveaway and although I always performed under the name of Xando, anybody in the business would know my real name. I paused, waiting for the uproar. It never came and I was led to the stage.

I played along as he relayed snippets of the fake background I'd given his assistant in the bar. Then a ghostly face began to coalesce from the rear of the stage and the sharp silence in the room cut into the air like fingers of ice. This seemed like the perfect moment.

"What's happening?" I called and I stepped forwards towards the table.

I caught the look in his eye as he realised I was moving too close to his set-up. "Wait," he said. "Don't move, the spirits are talking."

"Where?" I stepped forwards again and tripped, stumbling into the table with such force that one of the candlesticks wobbled then swung across the table, dangling crazily on the end of the wire which reached up into the fly loft.

"What are you doing?" the Great Geoffrey's command slipped.

"It's alright, I've got this," I said loudly. I fumbled with the

108

candlestick pretending to try to replace it but in reality, I was making it clear to all that it was suspended on wire. "It seems to be tangled. Hang on." I gave a big pull and the wire snapped. I stumbled again and tripped on the tablecloth, dragging it to the floor.

The Great Geoffrey stood in panic and raised his arms. "It's alright," he said. "Just leave it. Everybody, it's just a slip."

"I think I've dropped my PKE meter." I pretended to search the floor.

"What? Leave it. We'll find it after the show."

"It's alright. I've got a torch." I pulled my million candle power tactical special forces flashlight from my pocket, aimed it at the Great Geoffrey and switched it on.

He jumped, squealed and too late, flung his hands to his eyes.

"Sorry," I said and aimed the torch away from him and towards the rear of the stage.

The darkness which had quietly guarded its secrets failed under the onslaught of my million candles and two black clad helpers jumped in alarm as they were exposed to the house. They fumbled with their not-so-ghostly white-painted mannequin in a futile attempt to hide it from the light.

In another round of faked panic I swung the torch around the stage, bringing into the glare a full electric lifter under the table which was clearly slated to be used in a spectacular table levitation later.

Unhappy rumblings circled the hall along with cries of 'Fake' and 'Fraud.'

I turned to the Great Geoffrey. "I suggest you go back to card tricks."

I slid out of the theatre in the midst of the chaos and headed for home.

The following morning I bought all the local papers I could find and began making my lists. Mediums, spiritualists, palm readers and ghost hunters. I had no issue with them as such,

109

each to their own. But if they were going to prey on the bereaved and heartbroken then I was coming for them. All my years of creating stage illusions and conjuring tricks had given me a very special set of skills and Kev Blake was right. I shouldn't waste them. I was going to hunt down every charlatan, scam artist and flim-flam man and shine the light on them. No longer would they be able to hide in the shadows and fleece the vulnerable. Maybe there were spirits, maybe not. Who knows, one day Amy might even reach through the veil. But whatever was real or not real, there was going to be no room for the fakers to ply their nasty trade.

I had my mission and I was going to pursue it relentlessly But most of all, I was going to have fun.

Epilogue - The Banker

After the last story, the Banker looked at me and said, "I think I understand."

"Then your story has begun," I said.

He eased himself up from my cardboard mat and stretched out his knees. They clicked in protest.

He started walking away then paused as if he'd forgotten something. He turned. "Thank you," he said. He walked slowly across the square, heading for the underground station. His pace was unsure and he even stopped a couple of times as deep thoughts briefly stole his ability to walk. Eventually, the shadows of the underground entrance took him and he was gone.

The banker never returned to Friedman Square after the final story. About a week after he'd disappeared, I watched a postman wandering the square. Normally his path was brisk and direct, efficiently moving from building to building in the shortest time possible. Today, he drifted like the last autumn leaf in the dying trace of an evening breeze.

He noticed me and paused for a moment before heading in my direction. He arrived in front of me looking slightly lost and confused.

"I have a postcard," he said. "But it's addressed to the Storyteller under the statue. You a story teller?"

"I am," I said.

"Here, this must be for you." He handed me the postcard.

I examined the image on the front. It was one of those simple tourist cards showing a stylised map, this one of South West Cornwall. An arrow had been drawn on the card in blue ink, it pointed to St Ives. I turned the card over. A simple line graced the rear. "I have my story now, I'll give it to you when we next meet. It was signed simply, Tony.

I slipped the card in my pocket. I liked Cornwall, it would be nice to visit there again.

I realised the postman was still watching me. "That's definitely for you then, is it?" he asked.

I nodded. "Yes, a note from a good friend."

"So what's with the stories then?

Choices come,"I said. Stories are to be told and heard. Stay awhile, I'll tell you one."

Homeless

by Helen Garlick

15th November 2022

I am the eighth billionth person to be born on the planet. Planet Earth they call it.

They do not know who I am. I do not know my significance.

In fact, I know little in this moment, the moment before my next birth, in a caul in a faraway country in a place they'll tell me soon enough is home.

I have no home. I do not know what home is. I am nowhere. I am no-one. I could be anyone. I am someone. Everyone. I am everywhere.

In the end, the beginning.

Omega, Alpha. Alpha, Omega.

Who am I?

A weak wisp of smoke twists skywards from the wet bits of wood he's collected in the park earlier, hidden inside his trench-coat and now stacked into a little pyramid, a few extra sticks stashed at the side. The red lighter he'd spotted by the gutter earlier that day was a find. Decent. He'd held it in his left hand all day, tucked in, a promise of warmth he could, for once, rely on.

Flicking the lighter on again now, he squats down, wincing at the shooting pains from his left leg, to hold it beneath the firelighters he's rolled up from Metro sheets like his mum showed him how – always works a treat. The Metro front page had announced that today the eighth billionth person on the planet would be born. Poor sod, he thought. What a time to be alive. Will he, or maybe she, even have a planet to live on in sixty years' time?

He hunches over the fire, his back to the north from where the wind is trying to snuff it out. There's a nip in that wind. He's craving warmth, fearing a chill which will bite deep into his bones. The lighter's flame sputters, but it's enough for the smoke to splutter into a blue fire tongue, reflected back in his watery eyes, the wetness on his cheeks, which could be rain.

That'll do. He can work with that. He could splash some rum on the fire to make it light up better but what a waste. He feeds more sticks into the fire and the blue flame turns yellow, flickering orange, red. Then the smell of the acrid smoke catches him and he starts to cough, racking his body. It takes him several minutes before he can stop.

Wiping his mouth with a coat sleeve, he sees red smears and flecks and wonders how long he's got. Might be tonight, if he's lucky.

He stands up, stretching his six foot frame and unscrews the Captain Morgan bottle to knock back two slugs in quick succession. He never stops at one, one is never enough. Now he can drink the whole bloody bottle, no one to tell him different. The sweet brown liquid scorches, tumbling into his stomach, spreading a fake pledge of comfort.

Cheers, Cap'n. He tips the bottle up towards the dark night sky, turning his gaze heavenwards, searching for Polaris, the North Star, but it's still covered by clouds. This bloody weather, never stops. Rains even more these days, hard rain too. More like a monsoon. Climate change they call it. All those billionaires swanning round in those monster yachts. They should stop them for a start. Their greed makes his heart hurt, and he detests them even more because their yachts share the same ocean where his love lies deep.

Looking back towards the empty stack of a rolled up sleeping bag on top of cardboard he's collected, all neatly folded, he sees, right on top, the couple of blankets he was given a few weeks back, can't remember exactly when. She seemed nice, but she wanted me to come in to a shelter and then the interfering would start over. And the taunts. No way.

He's free here. He feels safer tonight. He's found a space behind the car wash, away from prying eyes where he can lie in peace. No one should spot him here tonight.

Trying to forget the memories from the last fortnight or so, he screws up his eyes. Big boys don't cry. Bangs of rockets, bursts of fireworks screaming to the sky, howlers they'd called them, had caught him out, bloody well set him off howling. He'd dropped in the gutter between cars, to shut out the noise, scrunching himself into a ball to fight echoes inside, yelling animal cries into his trench-coat, before the coughing started back up again.

He'd tried his best. The noise of the fireworks opened floodgates long shut, searing into the clouded skies of his mind pictures of his mate, Chris. He was the one who'd always had his back, his best friend, the only one he'd ever loved, though he'd never told him so. He could hear it, as if it happened yesterday, the sound of Chris crying, like a baby, 'I'm cold, I'm so cold,' before passing on, too bloody soon. And there's no earthly grave to mourn him.

Not fair, life.

Sniffing in a gulp of air, he drinks a few more measures. Of course, he could go to that place, a house, he won't call it home though he used to, to see his sister Dawn, the one to whom his mum and dad left their property. It's only a couple of miles away. He could even walk it, the leg might hold up for that. He can't blame them, Dawn was the one who looked after them all their short lives whilst he was the one who drank all of his life, well what was left of it after Chris went to the other side and he left the navy, medically discharged.

Poor old Dawn. She'd never had a life of her own, never the time to find herself a chap, and now it was too late. Fair enough, he could understand Mum and Dad's decision. What he couldn't stand was the look of pity in Dawn's eyes nowadays. It made him want to run away. They didn't talk much, at all really, but Dawn's stare told him what he needed to know about the choices he'd made in his life, the things he'd done. Or not. But it wasn't his fault.

Never mind. It should all be over soon.

Sixty's no age, they say, but it's long enough to cock up a life, proper job. Better this way. Dawn's enough on her plate. Tired her out, looking after Mum and Dad all those years and then them dying only one day apart. Enough for anybody to have to cope with. Not sure she's ever recovered.

Taking a last, draining swig of the Captain, he places the bottle on one side, next to the fire, reducing now to ashes. He brings over his sleeping bag and blankets, and arranges the cardboard underneath for his bed, near to the extinguishing fire. Shuffling deep down into the bag, he pulls the blankets hard over his head to wrap them tight around his present form. Allowing the skies of his mind to hover over the sea, he drops into waves of dreams. Forcing his left leg to crook in towards him, he draws in his knees, clasps his arms around his torso and buries his head into his body as, finally, he rounds himself, like an egg, into an O.

Somewhere on another side of the world, a baby is born in a caul. It's a rare occurrence: a one in eighty thousand chance.

The midwife says, 'Praise be, we've got a little mermaid here,' and then, seeing the cloud of worry shadowing her parents' faces, reassures them, 'Oh, that's just what they say when a baby's born in a caul. I've never seen it happen before. And doesn't she look beautiful?'

The parents both smile, beaming joy in the bliss of their firstborn's birth.

The midwife sees how calm the tightly curled-up baby is, still floating in her amniotic fluid, cloaked in her sac on the lying-in bed. Swiftly scanning her, the midwife sees that the baby has all four limbs intact, all twenty fingers and toes, although her left leg might be a little crooked. She makes a mental note to check that.

Proffering a crochet hook to the father, nodding towards the child, the midwife asks him to pierce the caul. As he does so, the baby is cast into the air of life. She takes her first earthly breath, with a cry and then a minute cough, before her breathing starts to steady.

The midwife studies the baby, tenderly wiping her with a muslin sheet and she grins. The baby looks in every way perfect.

'Well, as she's been born a mermaid, how about we call her Ariel?' the mother says.

Looking deep into his brave woman's eyes, the father nods, adding, 'And as she's our firstborn, we could also call her Alpha, perhaps, as a middle name.'

Picking up the baby, the father first cradles her in his arms before he gently hands her over to her mother's embrace, saying, 'Ariel Alpha, welcome to the planet. Welcome home.'

The Wall

by Mark Blackburn

Every night in Stefan's dreams The Wall grew bigger. As you approached it, it wasn't so scary. You came down West Street and there it was at the dead end of the road – a normal brick wall a few feet high topped off with concrete, and beyond was the sea. You could see the Isle of Wight off to the right on a good day, and there was the Nab Tower ahead – Stefan liked to pretend this was a ship, coming towards him. Or going away, depending how he felt on any given day.

Yes, so from the land side, The Wall wasn't so scary. But the other side fell down to the beach below, unforgiving shingle with stones the size of boulders. It was at least a six foot drop, and that was on a good day. Despite the size of the stones, the angry sea could whip them around like marbles, and after a storm the distance down was even more terrifying. Terrifying, because everyone else in the gang had jumped off the wall, and Stefan hadn't. Each passing day made him more of a coward, more of a target, and made the drop seem more impossible than ever.

It's not like the gang were mean or anything. Even if they did sometimes gently tease him about his accent, they'd accepted him in when he'd come down here with his mum after the house in Kherson had been flattened in the bombing. They'd fled Ukraine for the safety of the UK with only the clothes they wore and what they could carry.

There were about a dozen of them in the gang, some kids who lived there all year round, the rest were the 'blow-ins' who came to their holiday homes each year. Tony was the first to do anything, and the first to have jumped from The Wall. He'd fallen over and yelled when he landed, and they all thought he'd broken his ankle, but he soon stopped blubbing. He got up and basked in the glow of having been the first. Over the next few weeks everyone else had – even three of the posh Bunting sisters who lived in the biggest house on West Street. It was rather different from the flat on the main road out that Stefan and his mother lived in, courtesy of a distant uncle who ran the takeaway downstairs. His mum worked in there sometimes, and did other jobs around the small seaside town.

All of the kids' games revolved around the beach. At low tide they'd go shrimping, crabbing and rock-pooling, or just make patterns, dams and complex structures in the sand (don't insult them with the word 'castle'). When the tide was really far out because of the full moon or something, you could see old ruins miles out in the sand; hundreds of years ago there'd been a village right out there, but over the centuries the sea had crushed its way in, turning solid walls into mere limpet-covered foundations. It made Stefan think of the ruins back home in a wistful kind of way, as he wondered what they looked like now.

One evening after a fish and chip supper there was still some light in the salmon pink sky over the ocean. With the rest of the gang safely in their own homes watching telly, Stefan went out, crossed the town and pondered The Wall close up on his own. The drop didn't look too bad in the dusk; he considered jumping it there and then, just to get it done. But then he thought about it – there was no point, no one would see him do it, no one would believe him.

The next morning opened out to a glorious late summer day. Usually Stefan loved being here at the coast, free and full of friends, able to forget the horrible last days of life in Ukraine, and the better life he had before. But the other kids would NOT stop talking about The Wall, and how Stefan had to do the jump before the end of the holiday. They decided today was the day. The sun was shining, the tide was way, way out, the shingle was dry and there was no possible reason for him not to leap, at least as far as the gang thought. The baying chorus made clear he had no choice; it was time to jump.

He climbed up and shuffled to the edge. He could see the stones miles down beneath the toes of his Sports Direct own-brand trainers. The nylon shoes with their flimsy rubber soles aren't going to help, he thought. But then a chorus of "Jump, jump, jump," throbbed behind him. His time had run out. He jumped. The kids down below on the shingle saw him plummet, a loose bundle of clothes and limbs. He crashed onto the stones.

But that wasn't how it seemed to Stefan. To his amazement he didn't plunge down to be bashed against the rocks, his thin legs snapping like Twiglets. No, instead, a kind wind seemed to lift him up, and the shingle below shrank away. At the same time, the tide whooshed out, to reveal the foundations of the drowned buildings he dreamt about. It went out further than he'd ever seen, in real life and even in his dreams.

As he watched, the seaweed and the barnacles dissolved from the walls, which started rising again, forming whole buildings; their roofs materialised as well, and then there were people! People and dogs picking their way along the tracks between the little houses! The whole little town under the waves had come alive!

He kept looking for a while, just floating a few hundred meters above, and then he realised he was going down again; just very slowly and it didn't feel scary. Then a gentle warm mist started blowing in from the sea, and soon he could only see the tops of the roofs, then just a few pinpricks of light from a handful of scattered lanterns. And then it was all gone, and he was drifting back down to the beach.

The other kids, having merely seen him crash to the rocks, had run down the slipway behind The Wall and then slowed as they approached the slim form spread-eagled stock still on the shingle. To their amazement and relief, the figure started to move.

Stefan slowly opened his eyes, to see another pair of eyes

staring back at him; the deep sea blue eyes of Angie Bunting. He noticed there were specks of sea spray on the cheeks below them – or were they tears? "Oh my God, Stefan, we thought you were dead!" she cried, and reached down to hug him and pull him up at the same time.

"No, I'm fine", he said. "Just fine."

Another Day

by Tim Prescott

The quest begins on waking.

The quest for warmth, food and shelter.

The cold air breaks its way into consciousness and the nylon down comfort does not provide the safety of castle walls but only a bivouac of scant warmth.

Peeling the self from the cocoon it's hard to straighten up on legs shaking from fatigue and dehydration.

At least it isn't raining.

Put on the armour of the day and roll away the night into the pack, heave it to your shoulders, carry the world on your back.

Gathering the tools and weapons of the daily quest, a sword, a cup, a wand and coins. Those few coins gathered from yesterday's quest, not enough to break the fast with, just enough to rattle in the cup as like attracts like or so they say. Let's hope.

The first decision of the day is difficult to make on an empty stomach and head tired of dreams. Thoughts that now need will to action.

At least it isn't raining.

Somewhere quiet and safe lacks potential to earn. Attacks are less common with many witnesses. A compromise of numbers, no attacks with a lot of people around, more people, more witnesses, more witnesses, more pockets, more coins, but you're also easier to ignore, to walk past without even the turn of a head.

A shopping centre bathroom for morning ablution and mirror check on the swollen lip and broken tooth. Injuries sustained in an honourless confrontation. It wasn't even a confrontation; the word suggests an opportunity to defend. A cowardly ambush, a kick to a sleeping face from a last ordered wanderer with belligerent bravado he thinks will impress his friends.

A hazard of the homeless to be a target of those who actually have nothing to prove except their ignorance and cruelty. They wouldn't kick a dog.

The gum is starting to swell and ache and the scar. Well, that needs attention too.

The day's quest has begun, a search for food, shelter and dignity.

A site is claimed, a crossroads of footfalls and safety in numbers. A stall is set out. Magic wands of coloured chalk transform the concrete slab into a landscape to attract more coins into the cup. The sword is folded into a back pocket. It cuts through apple and plastic and nylon and could be brandished as warning in times of anxiety and threat. A fairly constant state. The sword stays folded.

At least it isn't raining.

"Every time a bell rings an angel gets its wings," chimes a coin into the cup, a token of hope, a smattering of kindness.

And so begins the quest for food reduced to affordable. Salt fat and sugar saviours to help keep out the cold.

Try to feel without feeling.

Emotions must be kept in check. Emotions are a drain on energy levels, emotions must be fed.

Pain. Pain is easy. Pain is pain like cold is cold, but lonely can be cold. Despair is like a hunger hollow, a deepening of the void at the centre of your being, like an empty stomach groaning for nourishment, a soul desperate for a word of comfort.

And heartbreak, feels like it sounds. A fragile cracking and falling in the chest, someone's fist around your heart pulling it free of the cushioned body that they might shatter it more completely.

And it is a they. People break hearts.

But the most common feeling is a far off thought of other things, better things, better times. Longing.

A long time ago, a long time to wait, a long way back and a long way to go.

Longing for something we cannot know but know it is different to what we have and have not today.

Food forage done a return to the pre-staked spot is not an option crowded out now by noisy others, others in gangs and groups, others all potential dangers. Slip into a side street when you don't want to be seen.

The pack is permanently on your back, a strolling fool open to experience when everything is new and fresh in this wide exciting world. But that's not how this feels. This is a diminished world, walkable from horizon to horizon in an afternoon that lasts forever, until, the knees tire and you need to sit. These shoes aren't made for walking.

At least it isn't raining.

The golden hour spreads light across the pre-twilight sky.

A new look-out post claimed with wand and sword and cup. A friend with more sustenance arrives. He had a good day and like he said, "at least it isn't raining."

Uniforms come but we're doing nothing wrong so we don't run and we don't hide. The interrogation begins with a question they call a welfare check.

Soft voices, open body language, but you can't help but notice the cap shrouded eyes and the bat-utility belt of weapon and restraint. Narrowed eyes, the hand goes to the belt. Stay neutral, stay sharp. A hand is raised and a card proffered.

"You need to get that looked at, they have a walk in clinic. You know where it is?"

No, we don't know where we're sleeping tonight, but at least it isn't raining.

Tom

by N. Joy

"It's lonely being a ghost.

Being a ghost is like being homeless. Like living on the streets. You are invisible to everyone except those in the same predicament.

We are just balls of energy really; we have no corporeal form. I think the reason we manifest looking like ourselves is because this is the last physical entity our souls remember. It's what we think of as us. Some display the scars and injuries of life and death, but most prefer to project the best image of who they once were. The 'them' they liked the most. Like me and Gloria.

We have built up communities, like we did when we were alive, first time. A diverse population, all with one thing in common. Life left us but we didn't leave life. We are still here sharing the same space; you just don't know it.

That's not to say there aren't scary ghosts, there are. They are the people who were mean in life, not welcome in Heaven but not wicked enough for Hell. Trapped in an eternal limbo. These do scream and wail like banshees, covered in their own blood, body parts hanging off. They like to scare, like teenagers' trick or treating as that's all they have left to do. They frighten me.

Then there are the crazy ones. The ones who go insane at the knowledge of their deaths. There are the ones who just refuse to accept it and the ones that don't even know they are dead, trying all day, unsuccessfully, to make contact. These are what you call poltergeists. They are unpredictable and tantrum like toddlers. They aren't mean, just confused but I try and stay away from them.

Not everyone stays. Some head straight for the light, others are dragged away from it. Some stay around for a few days, others for an afterlife. A lot must move on because there aren't that many ghosts, not for all the dead people there are.

I used to think a spirit was tethered to a person or place. We aren't. We can go wherever we want. Most stay close to the area where they lost their lives as they aren't ready to leave the familiarity and their loved ones, being not ready to sever the connection. I don't know why I have stayed.

Harry has been traveling for years. He's having more fun now he's dead than he ever did when he was alive. He pops back every now and then to regale us with tales of the sights he has seen. I may go with Harry one day, when I am brave enough.

There are groups of ghosts, like hordes of zombies. They cluster together at sites of great loss, drawn to the echoes of suffering like moths to a flame. Hundreds can be found wandering around aimlessly, puzzled by what happened to them, at places such as hospitals and battle grounds. I keep away from them, too, they scare me.

One of the worst feelings is when you think one of the breathers has seen you. In fact, they are disconnected from their own reality, daydreaming, staring right at you. Perhaps, for a second or two, they do see me, before rational thought blocks the view again. There are the occasional few, the gifted ones, who are willing to see or hear us. Like you. It's great when they do, but it never lasts. Once a channel is open any spirit can come through but it's the strongest and loudest that get a reaction normally. It's rare that I can communicate and have my small voice heard. I'm so grateful you are listening, but I know that you too, will have to go.

The reason we call you breathers is quite simple. Although, to you we are dead, to us we are not. We are not alive, but we are here. It is just a matter of perception really. We are living in a world that no longer sees us, has forgotten we existed. But we do still exist. Some breathers see us, like you. It's wonderful, to be seen or heard again, but it doesn't last, and we are on our own again.

I don't know why I'm still here. I don't know why I didn't go to Heaven. I tried to be a good kid. I think fate had other plans for me.

Gloria looks after me now, she looks after all of us. She attracts us like a beacon of hope. I don't know how she died; she says she didn't die she just moved on to a new place. I guess she was just old. Like me Gloria didn't have a family. She was abandoned at birth and raised by nuns. She never married. I like her tales about the children she used to look after. Gloria is like the granny I never had. Gloria was psychic in her lifetime and continues to help lost souls reach their final destination. She says I can help her. I have the gift, too.

My best friend is called Edwin. He's been here a very long time. We used to play together, before, but then I forgot about him. He dresses funny, like a little adult in jacket and trousers. He wears a strange cap pulled flat against his head. Eddie was murdered. He's OK now though. Our favourite game is hide'n'seek and we play dodge, Tommy taught us that.

I like Tommy. Tommy is older than me, nearly a man but not quite. Tommy was killed in a motorcycle accident. I often find him sat on someone else's bike. He says he's not ready to make peace yet, which is okay because Tommy is happy. He's always smiling and making mischief. I like it when he plays dodge with the breathers, he makes me laugh.

I hang around with Jill a lot as well. She isn't my girlfriend, she's too young! Jill died of influenza. When she isn't with me, she is at home with her elderly parents. They loved her so very much. I think they kept her grounded because they couldn't let her go. But as her family aged, she stayed their little girl, frozen forever in time. I think that she might go when they do.

There are lots of other people who live here too, like Roger,

126

Emma and Monty. They are nice. I don't know why they are here. I want to know but Gloria tells us we have to leave them alone. I like making up what happened to them. There are others too, like William, he's over there on the bench, has a limp. I pretend his leg was bitten off by a shark. Matthew, he's really tall, like a giant, might have hit his head on a plane. And Briony, she's really bouncy and giggly. Maybe she ate a can of worms? Not everyone here is nice. I hide from the mean ones when they come around.

I don't remember my death.

At first, I didn't know that I was dead, but I was really pleased I wasn't coughing anymore. I used to find it hard to breathe sometimes. I would have to go to hospital. I didn't like it, there were too many fuzzy people around me. I can run around as much as I like now, it's great.

When I woke up everything was the same, but different. I don't know how long I had been asleep. I was there but nobody could see me. In a house with seven other children you do become invisible, but this wasn't the same. I was confused and starting to get worried. When Taylor - he is, was, one of my foster brothers – walked through me I couldn't understand why I wasn't lying flat out on the floor. I was shocked I tell you!

I cried and cried. I felt a touch on my shoulder, I thought it was Taylor. It wasn't. It was Edwin. He took me to Gloria.

I think maybe I stayed because I am, was, am sensitive to spirit. Ever since I can remember I could see ghosts. They were fuzzier back then, like looking at someone through a bathroom window. I knew they were people, but I couldn't distinguish any detailed features. They didn't scare me or try to hurt me. They were just there, at the park, in church and around town when my foster mum dragged me shopping. I never saw any at school, I guess even ghosts didn't like school.

Like a lot of little kids, I had imaginary friends. I didn't realise they were ghosts until I met one again, on this side of life. My foster parents said they were happy friends in my head who would go when I made some real pals. And they did. I didn't have a family of my own. My mum died giving birth to me, and I never knew my dad because he never knew about me.

As I moved around homes, I found new friends in each, although Edwin always found me. There was Lily, she had long brown hair and blue eyes. And Chloe, she has hair short, but not like a boy. They were the first secret friends I remember. They liked playing tea parties. George, he wore a jumper that went up to his chin, and we used to play chase and climb trees. And there was Hannah and Amy and Toby, he had crazy hair the colour of an orange.

Toby was the first one I helped. Gloria helped, too. I found Toby at one of my old homes. It was his home, too before it was mine, but it fell down and squashed him. Toby was still scared of loud noises and would huddle against Gloria when it thundered. Tears rolled down Toby's freckled cheeks when he left, and he waved goodbye. He smiled and ran into the light.

Hannah found me again. Well, I found her hiding in a bush, but she found me first. Hannah was shy, she wouldn't visit me when my other friends came. I think she is seven, she is smaller than me. She has been here a long time. She was stolen away from her mummy and she never saw her again. I was so happy when she went into the light, it was the first time I had seen her smile.

I have become a ghost on a ghost hunt. I will find the rest of my friends and lead them on their journey. I think this is why I stayed.

Thank you for hearing me.
Goodbye."

The Bet

by Tom Barfett

It was all the result of the Celtic temperament, I suppose. I do not know how it really started or how the conversation came round to the topic; maybe it was because Patrick was an Irishman. In any case, when I went to see him on that May morning he was highly elated about something. It was obvious from the moment you entered the room that something had happened to him. One couldn't attribute his effusive welcome merely to the beautiful weather or to his temperament; there was more behind it than that as I was soon to find out. The conversation trickled along over our business, and when I should have hurried away, as I normally do, he insisted on my staying and drinking coffee with him. I thought this most unusual at the time, but as he was a good customer, decided to stay to humour him. It was over the coffee that he began to divulge the reason for the excitement which was bubbling beneath the surface: he had been dreaming. When he announced this I nearly replied in a derisive manner, and perhaps it would have been better for him had I done so. As it was, however, I humoured him and let him go on talking.

He had dreamt that he had seen the Derby, and he knew the winner. But that was not all, he gave the colours of the owner, and even said he recognised the noble lord leading in his horse. He was going to put his shirt on it and advised me to do the same. I had always reckoned that Patrick knew something about horseflesh, being an Irishman and all that, although I thought he was rather inclined to favour overmuch those from his own country. In his saner moments he would talk knowledgeably of sires and dams, staying power and hereditary ailments, and give an excellent reason for any tip he gave; and I must say his tips had won a good many people a spare pound or two. But this was really too much. Here he was suggesting that a horse, which at the last call over had been 66 to 1, would in a fortnight come home first in the Derby. It was all very well for him to say that of course it couldn't be done on the Epsom course, but the Derby was still being run in its wartime venue. He apparently knew all the answers. There was no gainsaying the little man. I couldn't persuade him that it was a foolish thing to do, to put all he possessed on a horse, dream or no dream. I left him as elated as I had found him.

I was worried about him for a few days after this, but with all the work that I had coming in at that time, I soon forgot all about it. Indeed, I might not have thought about it again had not my landlady announced on the day of the Derby that she was putting a shilling on the favourite. I am not much of a punter myself and would not even know where to start looking for a bookmaker, but she apparently had a friend who knew a man who accepted bets, which enabled her to place a modest shilling occasionally without losing anything of her suburban respectability. She volunteered to have a shilling put on a horse for me. This reminded me of Patrick's tip and as I thought I should lose my shilling anyway decided to put it on his horse. I learnt that the bookmaker accepted the bet very readily and not without derision. I was called away into the country that weekend and there was no radio where I stayed. I did not hear the result of the race and in fact forgot all about the shilling that had been wagered in my name, I was not allowed to forget it for long. "Why didn't you tell me you knew the winner of the Derby?" was my landlady's greeting on Monday morning. I was dumbfounded for a moment but then realised what she meant: my horse must have won. The truth was brought home to me when she handed me thirty shillings in place of the one I had given her to wager for me.

It wasn't until about a month later that I went round to

Patrick's office again. His car was not standing outside in its usual place when I drew up, and that seemed to me to be an omen. As I ascended in the lift a foreboding that all was not well came upon me. I could not understand this at all, but when I entered his office it appeared to have a somewhat derelict look and only his personal secretary was there to show me into the room marked 'Private'.

He was sitting at his desk with the summer sun streaming through the window, and I realised immediately that something must have happened. The light was glistening in his hair, which was no longer the colour I had known it but a gentle grey. He had a haggard look as though he had not slept for nights, dark pouches beneath his eyes betrayed his worry, and his lips usually so quick in repartee now seemed to sag and were slow to frame a reply to my salutation. Here indeed was a changed man. In place of the vivacious Irishman, there was a taciturn, rather sour, and aging figure, whose answers were given in an offhanded manner, and who seemed to have very little interest in anything at all. I finished my business quickly and he showed me out, without having expressed either pleasure or dissatisfaction at the results of our transactions.

It was not until some months later that I met a mutual acquaintance at the club, who told me the whole story. It appeared that he had taken out a large loan, using his house as security, to wager on his dream horse. At the last moment he was unable to visit his bookmaker himself and entrusted the money to a friend to put it on the horse for him. Unfortunately, the temptation was too great for the friend, who had disappeared from the country and had not been heard of again, leaving Patrick homeless.

In Chancery

by Lucienne Boyce

"The man who robbed the Mint! A good arrest, Mr Foster!"

The turnkey made an ugly gurgling sound. Though Dan did not join in the man's foolish laughter – the prisoner was going to hang and that was no laughing matter – he too thought it was a good arrest. Three Guardsmen, employed at the Mint to operate the heavy machinery used to stamp coins, had held a monier's apprentice at gunpoint and stolen four bags of gold destined to be turned into guineas. Every police officer in London had been hunting for the chief offender in one of the most audacious thefts in recent years.

Dan followed the turnkey past the taproom. The usual crowd of impoverished prisoners clustered around the door in the hope of picking up stray pennies by running errands for the luckier inmates of Newgate. Charity they could not expect. The revellers inside were already in fine voice, bawling lewd songs into the tobacco-heavy air.

In the porter's lodge, half a dozen prisoners had just been brought in on foot. A sad, bedraggled lot, they huddled together while they waited their turn to be called forward for their details to be entered in the prison register. It was a scene Dan had seen scores of times and he only glanced at it.

A woman broke away from the line and hurled herself at him. "Chancery!" She kicked and struggled against the warder who dragged her back, and clutched at Dan, screaming, "Chancery! Chancery!"

"Get that drunken slut out of here!" the turnkey snapped at the warder. "Sorry about that, Mr Foster."

"No, wait," Dan said. "Let me look at her."

The warder relaxed his grip, but did not let go. Panting and dishevelled, she stopped struggling and met Dan's gaze. She wore a faded, dirty dress; heavy, well-worn shoes that had been much repaired; and a scanty neckerchief that left much of her bosom uncovered. She looked exactly what she was: a woman who lived on the streets by whatever means she could.

"I'll speak to her," Dan said. "In private."

The warder looked at the turnkey, who nodded. They jostled the rest of the prisoners back into line and out of earshot, much to their disappointment.

Dan drew the woman to a corner of the room. "No one's called me that in years."

She almost smiled. "Chancery Dan. If I hadn't pulled you off that other boy, you'd have pulped him to nothing. Do you remember?"

Dan did remember. It was not long after he had joined the gang of children Weaver recruited from the streets with promises of food, drink, somewhere warm to sleep. And you did get those at first, in the rotten, cramped house in an alley behind Church Street in St Giles. After a few days, the old man set you to earning your keep. You learned to pick pockets, lift from shops, scramble through scullery windows while householders slept. If your skills didn't come up to Weaver's high standards, you were put out to whore. Dan's pickpocketing skills had been of the best.

He had earned the nickname Chancery when one of the older boys picked on him on his first night at the Warehouse, as Weaver's place was known. Thought he was a novice in these affairs, but Dan had already been living on the streets a year or more, since he'd seen his mother's gin-soaked body carted away by the parish officers. He had run away before the beadle got to him and turned him parish apprentice. He'd trapped the boy's head in one arm and pounded at it with his free fist. 'In chancery', the pugilists called the move.

There had been a girl standing by. She'd laughed and called

out, "Chancery! Let him go." He remembered her voice, so sweet and merry had it been, and her face still young enough to be pretty. It was her voice that made her living. On weekdays she warbled and danced bawdily about the streets, and on Sundays she raised her eyes heavenwards and trilled hymns outside the churches and chapels. Sometimes Dan and a couple of other boys worked with her, diving into pockets while she held the crowd's attention.

Now, with age and rough living, her voice had lost its sweetness and her face was hard and worn. Yet still there lingered in her eyes something of the girl who had looked out for him.

"And now you're a Bow Street officer. Who'd have thought things would turn out so well for you?"

But she did not speak grudgingly. Luck was luck, however it fell. Dan's fists had been the saving of him in more ways than one. He'd been spotted fighting by Noah Foster, a retired pug who trained boxers at his gym in Cecil Street. He had taken Dan off the streets, given him a home, and trained him to fight scientifically.

"What are you in for now, Meg?"

"Murder. But I didn't do it, Dan. A thief and a whore I may be, but I'm no killer. You know that, don't you?"

He didn't know it, not yet. "So why are you here?"

"Me and Jack the Sailor broke into widow Cooper's house on Dean Street night before last. The old lady's half-deaf so Jack went upstairs to see what he could nab. There was someone else up there. I heard him shout at Jack – who's there? – and then there was a scuffle and they ran down the stairs so I dived under a table. The man ran out of the house and Jack came after calling, 'The old lady's dead! Get out of it!' Then he was out the front door too, and I was crawling from under the table when the constables arrived. One of them gave chase, but Jack got away. The other one arrested me for beating the old woman to death with a poker. But I never touched her, Dan. Ask Jack.

He'll tell you. It wasn't me."

"I doubt his word would convince a jury. They're more likely to think Jack killed Mrs Cooper, and they'll hold you just as guilty."

"But I didn't do it, and no more did Jack. It was the other man."

"It's not much of a story, this tale of another man. What did he look like?"

"I never got a look at him. Jack saw him. He'll tell you." She clutched his arm. "You have to help me, Dan. They're going to hang me."

Gently, Dan put his hand over hers. "I'm not sure there's much I can do, Meg. The only thing that will do any good is finding the killer."

"Then you'll do that, won't you?"

"I can't promise anything…Where will I find Jack?"

"He usually sleeps at Higgins' lodgings in Dyot Street." She raised his hand to her lips and kissed it. "I knew you wouldn't let me down, Chancery."

It was late when Dan went to the St Giles lodging house, lantern in hand. There had been no point going before anyone had settled in for the night. The house smelt of cesspool, damp blankets, rotting food and filthy human bodies. The old, ragged man who collected the money for the landlord let him in and pointed to a door at the end of the grimy corridor. Dan ducked his head and descended the rickety wooden steps.

In the cellar, the smell was stronger, trapped between streaming walls and mildewed ceiling. The beams from Dan's lantern flared into a gloom lit only by a few scattered rushlights and guttering candle ends. Dan picked his way between the heaps of straw and rags. Lice-ridden heads shot up, bloodshot eyes blinked, hands flew to faces to shield them from the rays, or recognition. At first he got sullen stares and curses, but when they realised he wasn't going to leave them in peace until he had what he wanted, one of the lodgers pointed and grunted, sending him deeper into the chamber. There he was directed through an archway into a smaller, closer chamber, also packed with bodies.

"Bow Street officer. I'm looking for Jack the Sailor."

A bundle by his right foot shifted, a bony hand uncurled a finger, a man's voice rasped, "That's him."

Jack was lying on his side, his face to the wall. He was dead drunk and had not stirred when Dan called his name. He did not move when Dan prodded him, nor when Dan crouched beside him and shook him. His arm and head flopped to one side. Not dead drunk. Dead.

Dan turned him onto his back. A smell so foul that it penetrated even the rank air of the cellar rose from him: he'd died purging and vomiting. How had no one noticed the man's death agonies? His neighbours' stories were all the same: Jack had been there when they got in, for all they knew had been lying there all day.

Dan pulled a ragged coat over Jack's face. As he did so, a half-eaten round loaf rolled onto the dirt floor. The bony-fingered man grabbed it. Dan snatched it from his mouth.

"What's your bloody game?" the man snarled.

"He died of poison, and this is probably what killed him."

The next day, Dan went to Mrs Cooper's house. A stout, neat servant whose eyes were swollen from weeping let him in. She led him to a drawing room and asked him to wait while she told Mr Cooper, the mistress's son, he was there. A few moments later the man himself appeared. He was a tall man in his mid-thirties, still handsome but showing signs of fading youth in the flecks of grey in his thick black hair; the muddied complexion; the crinkling around the eyes. He had a distracted air, as well he might, frequently running a trembling hand through his hair.

"Principal Officer Foster? I had not sent for a Bow Street officer."

"I'm here all the same," Dan said. "It's a serious crime."

"Yes, of course. But I can't tell you anything more than I told the other officers. I came home from the theatre to a house full of constables and my mother...my mother—" He sank into an armchair and rested his head on his hand.

Dan remained standing. He took out his notebook. "Was anyone with you at the theatre?"

"Yes. We went to see Cumberland's *Joanna of Monfaucon* at the Theatre Royal and had supper afterwards."

Dan wrote down two names and addresses. "Did your mother have any visitors while you were out?"

"Only Mr Roberts. He came most evenings. He's an old friend of the family."

"Where will I find him?"

"He runs the Society for the Alleviation of Want Amongst the Deserving and Industrious Poor, on Castle Street. My mother was one of the patrons."

"And after Mr Roberts left, your mother went to bed. Was she alone in the house then?"

"Yes. She had given Mrs Dwyer the evening off to visit a sick relative. Mrs D's the housekeeper. She's been with us for years."

"I'll need to speak to her...I gather your mother was deaf."

"She was hard of hearing, yes."

"Deaf as a post," Mrs Dwyer said. "Though it came and went, depending on the circumstances, if you get my meaning. But she always had ears for a sad story and a plea for charity, did Mrs Cooper. Lord knows how much she's given to the Industrious Poor over the years. Well, she hadn't got anyone else to spend it on, had she? More coffee, Mr Foster?"

"Yes, please." Dan slid his cup along the kitchen table and the housekeeper refilled it. "What do you mean she hadn't got anyone else to spend it on? What about her family?"

"There's only Mr Samuel, but he'd run away from home,

hadn't he? Some idea he wanted to go on the stage. I ask you! Mr Cooper put his foot down, of course. 'You'll follow me into the business, my lad, or never spend another night under my roof.' No more did he. His father died while he was gone. Poor lad. He's hardly been back in his mother's arms six months and now this."

"You don't say so," said Dan.

"If you wouldn't mind waiting five minutes, Officer, while I just finish handing out these meals."

Dan leaned against the wall behind the table where a cheery, avuncular Mr Roberts and two grim-faced women doled out bread and soup. He looked beyond their backs to the noisy tables flanked by benches filled with ragged men, women and children eating the broth from wooden bowls. Most of them had proof of their industry tucked under their seats: trays of matches; bundles of straw for mending chairs; shoe blacking. One boy sat hunched over a crossing-sweeper broom held tight between his knees. How many had borrowed the paraphernalia for the occasion was impossible to say.

Mr Roberts ladled out the last helping, wiped his hands and turned away from the cauldron. "Well, now, Officer, I'm all yours. Let's go to my office, shall we? In you go…sit down, sit down, make yourself comfortable."

It was indeed a comfortable room, with armchairs, carpets, curtains, bookshelves, a fire in the hearth, and a desk with a leather chair where Mr Roberts seated himself. He pointed to a seat in front of him and Dan sat down.

"How can I help you in this tragic business? Do you not have the murderer in prison? A young woman, I believe. Sadly fallen, sadly fallen."

"Sadly fallen she might be," Dan said, "but I'm not convinced she did it. It seems there was someone else in the house."

"Yes, there was an accomplice who ran away, wasn't there?

Are you any closer to finding him?"

"He's found and he's dead…Could you tell me about your visit to Mrs Cooper's house that night?"

Mr Roberts sighed. "That fatal night. We played cards and drank tea, as usual. Samuel had gone out." He frowned. "To the theatre."

"You don't approve?"

"It was the theatre that lay at the bottom of all the trouble, Mr Foster. I've known Samuel since he was a boy. He was a jolly, careless little fellow. I never dreamed his light-heartedness would turn to viciousness. But it did, it did. He defied his father and broke his mother's heart when he ran away. We had no word of him for twelve years, until last September he turned up, footsore, half-starved, ill-clad. Of course, Mrs Cooper forgave him on the spot, and believed his tales of a life of struggle and hard work. But that was not the truth by a long way, Mr Foster, not by a long way."

"What was the truth?"

Mr Roberts folded his hands on his stomach and leaned over the desk. "Gambling, debt, and worse, Mr Foster; gambling, debt, and worse." He lowered his voice. "Burglary."

"Burglary?"

Mr Roberts sat back in his chair, the leather squeaking beneath him. "He is not a bad man at heart, you understand, but he is a desperate one. He owes money, and his creditors are threatening arrest and the debtors' gaol. He asked his mother for cash, but he couldn't tell her what it was for and she, not understanding the plight into which his recklessness had plunged him, told him he must wait."

"Wait?"

"Until she was gone, Mr Foster, until she was gone."

"I see. And Samuel Cooper will inherit everything, will he?"

"Unless she has made a will in favour of someone else, yes."

"Do you know if there is such a will?"

"It is not impossible. For all his parents knew, Samuel was

lost to them for ever. She never spoke of it to me, but I know she was careful in matters of business. She had learned the habit from her husband, a solicitor. But I fear that if Samuel discovers such a document and realises that he will not inherit, the temptation to destroy it will be too much for him. No doubt, given his financial situation, he is already looking for it."

"Do you know where she kept her will?"

"She had a bureau in the drawing room where she stored her papers."

"You've been very helpful, Mr Roberts." Dan stood up and put on his hat. "Perhaps I might trouble you further? If you could accompany me to Mrs Cooper's and point out the bureau, I'd be grateful."

"But of course, of course, Mr Foster."

"My mother is not yet in her grave and you ask me if I've been looking for her will?" Samuel Cooper ran his hand through his hair and tugged angrily at the locks. "Of course I haven't."

"Is that because you already know everything is coming to you?" asked Dan.

"Who else would it go to?"

"I don't know, but you had been away a long time, hadn't you? She may well have left you out. That would be awkward, given you're in need of money to pay your debts."

Samuel twisted in his seat and looked at Mr Roberts, who sat with his chin on his steepled fingers, sorrowfully regarding the young man.

"I told you that in confidence."

"Never mind that," Dan said. "I need to see that will, Mr Cooper, and I'd rather not go to the trouble of having to obtain a warrant. It wouldn't look good for you."

"Good for me?" exclaimed Samuel.

Dan met his gaze and said nothing.

The other man paled. "Look away, and be damned to you."

Dan pointed. "Is that the bureau, Mr Roberts?"

"It is," Roberts replied.

There was a delay while they waited for Mrs Dwyer to find the keys. When she had gone, Dan unlocked the bureau and rifled through the papers.

"No will," he said.

"What?" exclaimed Mr Roberts, leaping from his chair. "Let me see."

He shouldered his way past Dan and scrabbled through the documents.

"Were you expecting to find a will, Mr Roberts?" asked Dan.

"No, of course not. It's just that…that…Mrs Cooper was so careful." He swung round and faced Samuel. "You have taken it, haven't you?"

"I haven't been anywhere near the bureau. And why should I want to destroy my mother's will?"

"Because she had left all her money to Mr Roberts," Dan said. "But then you came home and she was about to rewrite it in your favour. Wasn't she, Mr Roberts? So you killed her before she had the chance."

Samuel was on his feet now. "How dare you speak to Mr Roberts like that? You will leave this house immediately, sir."

Dan ignored the interruption and fixed his attention on Roberts. "You'd intended to kill Mrs Cooper, retrieve the will for safekeeping, and produce it later. I'm guessing your original idea was to frame Mr Cooper for the murder. Then Meg and Jack the Sailor turned up and you had to leave the will behind. It suited you well enough for the blame to shift to them, but when I told you I didn't believe they were guilty, you went back to your first plan. You went out of your way to tell me about the will, and to make sure I knew about Mr Cooper's thieving and debts."

"Thieving?" Samuel stared at Mr Roberts in consternation.

"Well, it's true, isn't it?" Roberts snapped. "You committed a burglary."

"Because I was starving! I saw the open door, I went inside,

I took a damask tablecloth and I sold it for food. You said you understood my desperation…that there was no need for me to go back to Worcester and make amends to the family. You said you sympathised with me."

"Sympathised! You made yourself hungry and homeless by your own foolish and selfish actions. You had a comfortable home and a good living to look forward to, and you threw it all away. Every day, people come to me half-naked and hungry and with nowhere to sleep, through no fault of their own. People who work for the little they have, who struggle to keep themselves and their families. Mrs Cooper wasn't going to leave her money to me. She was going to leave it to my Society – to the *deserving* poor. Why should a wastrel like you have it?"

White-faced, Samuel staggered back, clutched at the bureau for support. "You killed her?"

"She told me there would still be something in the new will for the Society," Roberts said. "But it should all have come to me, all of it. And I knew if you found her proper will, you'd destroy it."

"Because that's what you'd have done in his place, isn't it?" Dan said. "But it seems Mrs Cooper had already destroyed it. You didn't know that when you beat her to death. And because Jack saw you, you killed him too. With your connections with the homeless, it was easy enough for you to track him down. Made it look like an act of charity too when you gave him one of those loaves you serve in your soup kitchen. Arsenic, wasn't it? As for Meg, all you had to do was let her hang. Why was that, Roberts? Weren't they deserving poor enough for you?"

"They were thieves!" Roberts's voice shook. "The Society was my life's work."

"It was their *lives*," Dan said.

Roberts was locked in a Bow Street cell, and Dan had visited Meg and told her the murder charge had been dropped. She would still have to face trial for burglary, but as she had not carried off any goods, she would probably be acquitted. A thorough search had confirmed that Mrs Cooper's old will had gone, and though she had not lived long enough to make a new one, Samuel would inherit as her next of kin. There was nothing left to do but go home.

But Dan did not go home. The abandoned Warehouse was a ruin now, the roof caved in, the windows empty of glass, the doors hanging on their hinges. He pulled back the board nailed over the front door and made a gap large enough to squeeze through.

It was dark and still inside, the only sound the scurrying of rats over the rotten floorboards. In that corner, he remembered, had stood the table behind which Weaver sat to examine the goods the children delivered to him at the end of the day. His stick lay on the table, within easy reach, in case proceeds fell short.

Beyond that door was the room where Weaver retired to discuss business with thief-takers, pimps and footpads. Upstairs was the storeroom, filled from floor to ceiling with handkerchiefs, watches, jewellery, clothes – all the things Dan and the others had stolen – to be sorted and fenced. Down those steps was the cellar where they slept. Where Dan had gripped a bully's head in his arm and punched him while a girl stood by, laughing.

Dan set his back to the wall and slid down to the floor, his hands on his knees. He could almost see the boy he had been in front of him, almost hear the girl's voice in the darkness.

Let him go, Chancery. Let him go

Tried

by Colin Leamon

Sometimes you end up on the street through no fault of your own, though sometimes you've only got yourself to blame, and this is what Charles Wyatt knew only too well, but it could've been so much worse. As the man had asked him to, he remembered, castigating himself for the umpteenth time for not taking a closer better look, taking the safer way out and not chasing what he had lost, yet he'd not listened to that voice in his head.

It was years ago when the old lady had approached him. How Charles, a frail, greying wisp of a man, past his sell by date, wishes he had taken a more careful look at the elderly lady who had brought him this book; just to be sure, before he put his foot in it again, he recalled, cupping the tea in his hands encased in a cheap pair of gloves, trying to stave off the biting cold.

After all the years of fluffing he'd come to doubt his first impressions. Yet he had, even if he double questioned it, come to recognise the homely features and eccentricities his producer wanted to put on the telly, as if anybody else called it that these days, if only he could stop second guessing himself. Yet, she fitted the bill too well, like an actress playing a part, but she might be real, he convinced himself; but what did he care? He'd get a spot on the programme when it went out. He'd be back on Channel 9! He had been on Channel 9 though no one believed him; he was a homeless bum who'd lost his marbles. Channel 9? Ha!

"Sorry, where was I?" he muttered to this bloke who'd bought him the hot drink, with a cold sandwich and bag of crisps. Getting warm took priority. "Yes, Roadshow Antiques.

I hadn't been featured on it much the past few seasons as no one had any more time for printed works anymore; artefacts of the past nobody collected lately, it was all online. Sodding computers!"

His tummy rumbled, Charles couldn't wait any longer. He took a hungry bite. The chap said he wasn't in any rush. Charles was ready to recount the memories of that day. He thought back, a wistful expression on his face, to the book. Yes, the book.

"This book was special, I could almost feel its power through my fingers; the paper the words were printed on was ludicrously thin, its binding battered, and corners had been folded over. It had been loved."

Charles looked up, "How I'd hated it when books were presented to me for my expert evaluation in pristine condition," he mumbled through a mouthful of bread, cheese, and ham.

The man agreed, it defeated their purpose. Now, all that Charles' scholarly talents told him, were what had once been in the burger from the wrappers he stole from the bins.

"I'll never forget… She was an elderly silver-haired lady, lines of experience etched on her face and I recalled our conversation."

"May I ask how you came across this, please?" I'd asked her.

"It was my great grandfather's. It's been passed down from father to son. It was my husband's," she'd said with the slightest of accents, one I couldn't quite discern.

It seemed innocent, and going by the date of publication it added up; if it was new when the great grandad had got his hands on it, which was neither here nor there, it made me less cautious. If my suspicions were true I'd be famous! It would be a pity to watch this doting old lady publicly executed, but I would be famous and books might be prized again for a while before the next fad stepped in. Charles let his thoughts wander. The guy really wasn't in any rush; he'd sought him down; he could wait. He didn't really know the man's occupation or what he was up to. Charles didn't think any more about that.

Going back to the woman... In his mind, Charles told himself her age wouldn't affect how little she would suffer getting shot, though how it most definitely would, if other more gruesome methods were called for, but then it would be quicker. It was not as if she had many years left in her, he reassured himself. "And I'd be famous!" He went on without missing a beat. He was rather famous once, riding the wave of nostalgia some fifty years ago when he could charge exorbitant prices for public appearances, where he was treated like royalty by vulgar commoners, minus twenty percent. He missed those days.

"Do you happen to know the language it's written in?" I'd asked.

"I'm afraid I don't. Would it affect the price?" she queried.

The sandwich was now gone, the tea was still warm, the ready salted crisps would be my dessert.

Charles saw how these last words made a dent in her mask; to ask this early told him her motives, unrehearsed and unedited, and un-staged? Would it go in her favour in court? That she had no idea what this thing was?

She continued, "That's why I want to sell it, to be honest. It's just hanging around gathering dust. My granddaughter's getting married, I'd like to maybe give her a little for her honeymoon."

That silly old cow then went and rambled on about this relative and how nice the boy was, and I'd let her talk without interruption. On the black market this book would buy me a first class 10-year cruise to the outer planets, a mansion on Earth, where the land was more valuable than any building built on it, and very much more besides.

"You never thought to have it translated?" I'd asked.

"That's the funny thing; Marion, that's my late husband, said it was cursed but was too afraid to get rid of it, something about Hell and damnation so he hid it under the floorboards and made me swear to never tell another living soul about it but he's dead, now and I'm too old to believe a word of that."

It was true. In the years after their general ban at the start of the last uprising, books were burned across the world but when this ruling became a hate crime to even own one, the prices skyrocketed to meet collectors' demands. But this book was special.

Should I have called for the cameraman to come over? Was the lure of fame so attractive? Charles drifted away for a moment.

"Go on," prompted the bloke who was an undercover policeman.

"I'm no linguist but just as a book in this condition I'd say between nine and twelve hundred."

"As much as that?"

"Yes, but if trends change you might get up to eighteen hundred at a collectors' auction."

"I don't think I'll be around by then, do you, Mr Wyatt," she had said with aplomb. "Doesn't what it's about matter?"

"That's what's concerning me. At the moment it's just a book…"

"They're not banned anymore. My dad told me how his father would tell him all about life back then," she interrupted, adding, "It's not a fake."

Another oddity. Fake, it was a relative term, books had been printed after the regime had fallen, for a short while, it was only books published before those dark days, which counted.

"No, it's pre-2246, I'm sure of it."

I'd made my mind up. I indicated to the cameraman, sealing her fate. I would be famous. How I could've stolen it off of her for that eighteen hundred, that was the scam; give a baiting estimate, follow it with a potential price, then pay that price and everyone would leave happy. All of us experts were in on it, our goons mingling amongst the crowds spying out potential suckers. Pay him, pay off the cameraman, pay off the security and give the producer his cut. 'Up to eighteen hundred'? It being 'just a book'? It was worth almost double that, but not this!"

"Hello, Kelsey," the 'old woman' had said to the cameraman. Damn! The truth hit like a hammer, only from the inside out. I'd been 'Tried'.

Charles Wyatt knew who he was; he had been telling his story, giving hope that one copy still remained. Who was the expert, eh? Not her! She didn't know what she had.

He knew now what to expect. He had to be silenced.

The cop stood up, pulling out his gun. It sure didn't matter there were loads of people to witness it, record it; not for many decades had that mattered.

Living on the street; it could have been worse? Whilst you're still alive there is always hope; a chance tomorrow might not be any worse than today and another day closer to when the man in the book might keep His promise, but not today.

"Even traitors to the state get a final meal." His was a sandwich and a packet of crisps.

"Of course, it's a fake you blithering idiot!"

It was the law. He'd lost his job, his wife and everything else money could buy you these days.

He looked into the man's eyes with a sense of peace; he might've been a selfish son of a bitch a long time ago, but he had changed. He closed his rheumy eyes and passed into eternity as his brains were blown out with these final words ringing in his head.

"Of course, it's a fake you blithering idiot!" she'd said again, as the part she played fell away. No Bible has been seen in over two hundred years."

The Veteran

By Elizabeth St.John

"You ain't from around here." The man lurched at Frank, emerging from the small crowd blocking the alley to Charing Cross.

A fire heaped high with rubbish and a broken gate belched an acrid yellow smoke that hung in the chill evening air. Through the haze, Frank glimpsed the river, black and leaden under the oppressive cold. At the passage's end patrolled two watchmen, standing stiffly and talking easily. Probably ex-military too. They'd chosen one path after the war. He'd taken the one less travelled.

"Is anyone?" Frank replied, standing his ground. The man's northern accent didn't belong either.

He grunted. A livid red scar snaked across his mangled face, puckering an empty eye socket. "Where you going?"

"Just around."

"Where you been?" A couple of men broke from the group under the archway, limped towards them.

"Just around." Frank repeated. He heard his own educated accent, dialled it back. "Like you."

The men stank, their leather jackets sweat stained, clothes filthy from living rough. Their leader glanced over his shoulder, saw his own suspicion reflected in their expressions. "Turn back. You ain't got no right to go through to Westminster."

A protest rose in Frank's throat. Once it had been his world. He had spoken before parliament. Ratified leadership's decision to go to war. When he first returned, he tried to find himself in the banquet hall and meeting rooms, the great abbey walls. He wanted to feel at home there again, be himself before he became lost in the carnage of defeat–and the alcohol he used euthanized his feelings. He had wanted to remember a previous life, relive his own optimism and desire to defend his country. Now he found his purpose in men, not monuments.

Frank stepped forward, and the men gathered closer. "I have my rights."

"You 'ave your rights." The man hawked and spat, the yellow glob narrowly missing Frank's boot. "And I got mine too. And right now, I'm telling you to piss off."

Laughter rocketed about the burly men. One of them kicked a glowing timber back on the fire, and sparks exploded into the darkening sky. Frank sighed. It was always the same. These men were feral, had no doubt been on the move for months, if not years.

"Look, you don't have to be here. I can offer you a place to stay. Money to tide you over." He rummaged in the pocket of his greatcoat, the coat that proclaimed his own military background.

The leader took a step closer.

"You think money and a Guards' coat is getting you favours? You could've got that anywhere. Turn back, mate. We took care of England's future"—triumph coloured the man's words— "and you look like you sold out." He drew a knife from his belt and let it hang at his side, glistening menace in the firelight.

Darkness shrouded the pavement just feet away. The streets had swiftly emptied. The watchmen had moved on from the end of the street. The last of the pubs by the river emptied out. A shout in the distance. A door slamming shut. And the incessant, overly loud crackling of the fire.

Frank reached out his hands to show they were empty. "*Honi soit qui mal y pense*,"

The man whipped round. "What you say?"

"Shame upon he who thinks evil of it." Frank murmured.

The man peered at him in the falling darkness. "Why did you say that?"

150

"Because I'm a Guard too. And I want to help you, brother."

"You're a bleedin' do-gooder." The man pulled a flask from his other pocket, raised it to his mouth with a trembling hand. "I don't want your help."

Behind him, the others had lost interest, gone back to the fire. One of them opened a pack, threw a scrap to a lurcher lying on the ground next to him. They sank back into themselves, pulled their coats over their heads until they were shapeless forms, lying on the ground like discarded rubbish.

Frank took a chance, clasped the man's palm with his own. He felt a bony wrist, the sinews cabling the back of his hand.

"You may not want it. But you need it. Just like I did."

The man was silent. Frank could see he was trying to understand Frank's intent. Struggling with a touch that was compassionate, not antagonistic.

"Wotcha mean?"

"I was one of you."

"No you wasn't, not with that accent."

"Captain Frank Howard. Grenadier Guards."

The man fell silent.

"I fought. I came home." Frank took a deep breath. "And found it a foreign land. My wife had run off with my best mate. Took the kids. Didn't pay the rent, so I had no place to live..."

The man looked up at Frank. Recognition mingled with the glint of tears in his eyes.

"...except the streets."

The man shifted his knife, flicked it in the light. "You look all right now." He raised the blade higher, taunting Frank.

"It took a while." Frank ignored the veiled threat. "And a lot of courage. Dutch courage, we call it. Looks like you know the taste."

The man took another swig from his flask, buttoned and unbuttoned his coat, shuffled his feet. Frank knew that ploy. He was interested, curious. Just didn't want to admit it.

Frank took a step closer. "Come with me," he said. "Come

where I found my first hot meal in years, my first clean shirt."

"Where's that then, the palace?" the man replied. "They ain't got time for us. We served. And they forgets we even exist."

"St. Dunstan's Church," Frank said. "They've got a soup kitchen. They're good people. The priest there was a military man himself. He knows our type."

"I gave up on God a long time ago. He gave up on me."

Frank shrugged. "That's your business. Come on. Walk with me, soldier."

He turned, intentionally clicked his feet side by side before stepping out in a swift march. He tried not to falter, did not look back. Would habit and training overcome fear and mistrust?

Away from the blaze, the rancid London air drifted easterly cold and river dank. The chill crept into Frank's bones. He felt, rather than heard, the man fall into step beside him. Frank slowed his pace, still a march, just not the speed to get from Whitehall to the Tower in an hour.

Already the curfew bells rang out, and if they were to be safe at St. Dunstan's before the watch patrolled, they must hurry. The streets belonged to Cromwell, and they needed no encounters with the enemy. They had fought enough on the battle fields of Edgehill, Newbury; fled Worcester's defeat and run.

At the end of the Strand, by Temple Bar, the candles of St. Dunstan's Church flickered. Flaming torches cast a ragged icy path across the dark street. They were almost there. Safe for now from Cromwell's patrols. Safe for a night, enough time to draw breath.

Frank took the man's arm, and together they marched up the steps to the warmth of the shelter. Another man saved from the debris of a war fought on the battlefield of forgotten heroes. Another hope for a new life. Another homeless veteran brought in from the streets.

*****

The English Civil War, fought between 1649 to 1660, pitted cavaliers against parliamentarians, neighbours against neighbours, brother against brother. At its height, thousands of men died and thousands more were terribly wounded. The Grenadier Guards were raised in 1656 to protect Charles II. At the war's end, many of these valiant soldiers were homeless, their villages ruined, their wives and families killed or fled. Classed as vagrants, very few of these returning men were welcome, and even less were able to receive reparation for the time spent fighting. They were chased from town to town, with nowhere to live but the streets and fields of England's shattered countryside.

In 2023, the Royal British Legion estimates there are 6,000 homeless veterans in the UK, and while the number of veterans sleeping rough isn't 100% clear, most estimates place the figure at around 3% to 4% of the rough sleeping population. As veterans represent around 5% of the overall population, this means that veterans are actually proportionally under-represented in terms of homelessness statistics.

Everyone's homelessness journey is unique. However, specific populations such as veterans are especially vulnerable and isolated. On average, because they struggle to trust people who have no military background, it can take a veteran nine years to ask for help.

Not Just Anyone

By Richard Williams

Mary called it a summer house but everyone else knew it was a shed. It was bigger than your average shed, admittedly but the windows were all plastic and the sill was a mess of old cobwebs and dead flies. Craig had moved most of the garden tools to the building which Mary was happy to call 'the shed' but William still had the lawnmower for company which seemed larger and grander than the patch of wispy grass at the back required. But then there was much about the domestic life of his son and daughter-in-law that he didn't understand.

When Craig had brought Mary home from university one Easter, Brenda had been delighted that he'd found someone so 'motivated' to be his girlfriend. Craig was too laid back....like his father. William just remembered the relief he felt that his late wife had been such a generous and capable host. She had not been phased by the awkwardness of Mary's vegan indignation but responded to every pointed finger with kindness and diplomacy. As the whirlwind finally departed, they had clung to one another like rescued sailors back on dry land and he'd again professed his total love and admiration for her.

Looking back, he knew that he had relied on Brenda too much. Her willingness to manage every aspect of household logistics had been tacitly accepted for years and left him free to focus on his teaching and the church choir. He wasn't sure he even knew how the boiler worked or what flowed through the pipes. After the first diagnosis, he had wanted to take more responsibility but she was determined to carry on doing everything, lest any slowing down be seen as a sign of giving in. Keeping up with the exam marking whist coping with the potential loss of his lifelong love and support left little mental space for unravelling the mysteries of the washing machine control panel or learning how to cook his favourite lasagne.

In those final days, she had written multiple and detailed instructions and tried to explain how to pay which bill from what account but he had taken little of it in. His world was a dizzy carousel of doctors' appointments, well-meaning visitors who stayed too long and rehearsing obscure Latin anthems. She with no future thought of nothing else whilst he found himself wallowing in the best bits of the past.

Initially, after she died, he managed pretty well. He survived on ready meals and the extra portion of the Crabtrees' dish of the day. Craig rang each evening and a different member of the choir would appear claiming they were just passing when it was obvious they were operating to a meticulous rota. The school gave him time off, colleagues sent floral condolence cards and his best man offered a week in their timeshare cottage. But time moves on. Craig kept apologising that he hadn't rung since last weekend, Barry, the tenor soloist, seemed to be the only chorister ever in the vicinity and the school were sympathetic but the needs of the pupils had to come first.

He had no intention of giving in or giving up but grief overwhelmed him like a tsunami every hour of the day. He slouched unshaven on the sofa in his woolly blue dressing gown going through holiday photographs from Devon, North Wales and the 'once in a lifetime' cruise to America and the Caribbean. They had re-mortgaged the house to give Craig and Mary a substantial deposit on their 'must have' property and to raise funds for Brenda's mother's care home fees. They had borrowed another ten thousand for the cruise because his wife said they should spoil themselves as well as other people. He'd been worried about the financial commitment but Brenda's vases and lampstands were selling well locally and all his colleagues were sure he'd get the deputy headship. The potter's wheel stopped turning soon after she became ill and Joe Savage got the job earmarked for him even though he'd only been at the school for six months.

Anyway....none of that mattered now. In truth, losing out to the younger man and then being unemployed was a trivial annoyance compared with having his home taken away. He tried to follow what the first arrears letter said but it made no more sense than the central heating clock. He didn't read any of the others. Mary had tried to put things in order the one time she called round after the funeral but she got angry when the wine stain on the carpet proved too stubborn and she stormed out. It hurt him how quickly the sympathy of his friends and loved ones turned to impatience. For everyone else, it was four months ago. For him, it was always only yesterday. Craig finally took him to see a solicitor but by then it was all so late and he was too exhausted to put up a fight.

Most things went into a skip. There was only space at his son's for a few essentials. Craig had offered him the 'small bedroom....for a few....well until you're back on your feet, Dad.' William thought this an odd phrase. It was if homelessness was an illness from which, given time, you recovered. Maybe it was. Most of their memories had been crushed and buried at the landfill site and the disappointment Brenda would feel about him surrendering their home of thirty-two years was so painful, he would often walk a detour to avoid the house and being confronted with the shame. He sold his car to his nephew for half its worth so at least there was no overdraft...for now.

For the first few days with Mary and Craig, everything went well. He had hardly seen the twins since the wake and he was still fit enough to play on the floor and to read stories to them in amusing voices. Even Mary smiled once or twice. But his bouts of sobbing made everything awkward and it was soon clear that she wanted him up and out straight after breakfast.

She started giving him packed lunches and on rainy days, she reminded him that there was always the library. He took to washing in the public toilets because the bathroom always seemed occupied. He overheard the word 'smelly' being said as the arguments between his son and his wife became louder and more frequent. The children seemed more wary of him now. He went to his bedroom straight after dinner and read his old football annuals….the one 'luxury' to survive the eviction cull. He didn't sing with the choir any more. God hadn't responded to his desperate pleas for his wife's recovery so their relationship had abruptly come to an end. He was lethargic, miserable and more distant so the conversation, when it came, was not unexpected.

'Now that it's getting warmer, Dad and….Well you can have my thick sleeping bag. I'll bring your meals out on a tray and you can use the outdoor loo.' William had neither the strength nor the self-respect to argue….even though he had calculated one evening that his money had probably paid for all the bedrooms and possibly the garage. He pulled the 'cruise suitcase' across the muddy lawn whilst his son carried the rest of his worldly goods in two reusable Lidl bags. 'There's a double socket,' he said with scarcely concealed embarrassment, 'so you can plug in the heater…but don't leave it on overnight. We wouldn't want anything to happen to you.'

William had been in the summer house for a month and despite the best efforts of the dented radiator, the patched-up sleeping bag and his thermal underwear, he was forever cold and miserable. Hot meals were scarcely tepid by the time they'd crossed from the 'farmhouse kitchen' to his living quarters and the waiter barely stopped for a chat. His trips to the park (good day) and the library (bad day) had continued by force of habit despite no longer being the unwanted house-guest but the stares of young mothers and bespectacled librarians became ever more suspicious. He felt guilty although he wasn't quite sure why. When he tried to strike up a friendly conversation, the response was universally negative or hostile as if this was all part of a cunning plan to steal a child or run off with the latest audiobook. His bank account was almost empty but he was too proud to ask the Council for help and he doubted whether he was eligible. It was entirely his fault, after all.

After another restless and fruitless night of trying to divine Brenda's guidance, he decided to leave. His continued presence on any part of his son's property was causing offence and it was making him ill. He wasn't sure where he would go next but he had a vague idea about a shelter in the centre of town. William's future used to be calculated in terms of retirement and pension milestones. Now it stretched no further than the next meal and the sleep after that.

He crept away quietly soon after dawn without saying the goodbyes which would belittle them all. He couldn't carry the annuals so he left them for Callum with a smiley face on a post-it note. He put a £5 note for Emily in an envelope which had contained his farewell paragraph from the Chair of Governors. The suitcase would have kept his clothes dry but one of the wheels was wonky so he divided his clothes, his washing stuff, a water bottle and Tupperware box of shortbread biscuits between the shopping bags and a small rucksack, which Mary had used for her bronze Duke of Edinburgh award.

William had learned to treasure the days when it was dry and warm and he made good progress towards a recreation ground in the next parish. He figured that there would be less staring if he was not known. His anorak was fairly new, he was almost clean shaven and he could be regarded as a fatigued shopper taking a rest before continuing their weary walk to the bus stop. It meant a longer trek back into town to the shelter but it would give him another reason for filling those never-ending hours. By the time he reached a wooden bench overlooking two swings with cracked plastic seats, he was very tired. He couldn't even raise a faint smile in response to that of the young lady sitting at the far end, smartly dressed in a royal blue jacket, blonde hair escaping from a beanie hat as the wind started to get up.

'Mr Cooper?' William knew the voice but not the face. 'It's Maddie Painter. You taught me history and RE.'

'Oh…Maddie…yes.' He didn't look up.

'Are you alright, Mr Cooper?'

'I'm fine, thank you, Maddie. I'm just a little weary.'

She didn't reply as he still made no attempt to look at her. He stared blankly at a pigeon which was jousting for a crust of white bread with a tenacious blackbird just inches away from his feet. What would Brenda say?

'I'm sorry, Maddie. I'm being rude. How are you?'

'I'm good, Mr Cooper, really good. I'm going to Manchester University in September….to study history.'

He raised his head for the first time as he remembered her more clearly. She shuffled closer to him, her eyes bright with the enthusiasm with which she used to hang on his every word.

'Me…university? Mum couldn't believe it. The first in the family. It was all down to you, Mr Cooper. I hated school and was always in trouble until you became my teacher. You made the Tudors come alive and as for the Crusades!' She came to an abrupt halt. She had noticed the Lidl bag containing the pile of threadbare socks and underpants. She looked into his eyes and she knew.

'I'm very pleased for you, Maddie. You always had it within you. I just helped you untap your potential, that's all.'

'No..no, Mr Cooper. You were so much more than that. You were the first person who ever thought I could make something of myself. You told me to reach for the stars and that's where I'm heading.' Without thinking, she reached out and clasped his hands in hers. He thought he should perhaps pull away but the unexpected kindness and softness was too much and he just burst into tears.

At first, she felt awkward and looked hastily around to see if anyone was watching. And then her mind was clear. This was

Mr Cooper, her mentor, her inspiration, her life-saver... and now it was her turn! She gently rested his hand on the bench and pulled her mobile phone from her jacket pocket. She stood up and walked towards a newly planted sycamore tree as she dialled. She paced back and forth and waved her arms about as she spoke. By the time she returned, William had stopped crying and was blowing his nose on an old checked handkerchief that used to poke out jauntily from his suit pocket as he strode vigorously around the classroom.

'You're coming home with me, Mr Cooper.'

He wiped his nose one last time and gazed up at her, sheltering his eyes from the strengthening sun. 'No I couldn't....I wouldn't...I mean it's very kind of you, Maddie but...'

'But nothing. I've spoken to my Mum and you can have Gran's old room. It's just stood empty since the day she died. She had her own bathroom so you'll have your privacy. There's only Mum and me so it will be quiet....well, apart from when Question Time is on. Mum can get quite carried away but you'll like her and she insists you stay with us. We both do.'

William went to respond but the erudite historian was lost for words. 'I'm just..I'm just....'

'You're not 'just' anything or anyone. You are Mr Cooper, the most smartly dressed, funniest, most hard-working, worst car parking, best teacher ever. That's who you are and who you will ever be. Now come on. It's not far. Give me one of those bags.'

Without waiting, she grabbed the rucksack, slung it over her shoulder and began striding down the path towards the gate. William rose to his feet with a little more energy than before and followed a few steps behind. For the first time in a while he smiled to himself. 'I'm not just some homeless anyone. I'm William James Cooper, widower of the utterly incredible Brenda Elizabeth Cooper and I am, apparently, the best teacher in the entire world!'

Domino

by Elizabeth Revill

Karl Simons swore as he struggled to replace his butcher knives in the correct slots, "Bugger!" He tried again, using both hands to guide the steel blade into the block. The concentration for such a simple task began to show and a ball bearing of sweat bounced, bursting on the chopping board.

"Nesta!" he screamed, "Meat's ready for packing."

His wife lumped out of the cold room her more than ample body thudding along the saw-dusted concrete floor like a miniature earthquake. Karl eyed her with distaste, staring at the mass of wobbling flesh he knew was hidden under the voluminous garment which covered her from neck to knee. Her pastry-dough face was flushed.

Her size, however, belied her speed as she deftly sorted the cuts of meat, packed and sealed them before slapping on the price ticket and placing them in the cold cabinet. This was all done in stone, bitter silence without even a glance at her husband. The task done she plumped out of the shop into their private quarters.

Karl swept up the lumps of fat and gristle and checked the clock. He strode purposefully to the door turning the sign from open to closed. Early closing day - now was his time. Nesta wouldn't miss him. Ever since he'd lost his eye she couldn't bear to look at him. Not that it worried him. They hadn't had a proper relationship for years. They tolerated each other and yet there had been a time when they couldn't get enough of each other, would laugh hysterically at nothing and then laugh even more at the mystified looks of those around them.

Three children later Nesta had put on too much weight and

the magic was gone. Karl needed to find another outlet, another way of putting excitement into his life. This is when he decided to embark on his other career. He'd always been fit, agile and he had a strong sense of right and wrong. It was odd that burglary had become such an important part of his life.

Karl wasn't a common housebreaker. He wasn't a burglar who stole to line his own pockets. He was a thief with a difference. He liked to think of himself as more akin to those romantic heroes from fiction like, Raffles or The Baron. In becoming a burglar Karl tried hard to put right things, which had once gone wrong.

He sighed heavily, was he ever going to be able to return to his passion? For a passion it had become, as important as life itself. His disability affected his spatial awareness. How could he abseil out of buildings when he couldn't even get a key in a lock!

Mrs Gravely had been in the shop this morning, complaining how she'd been robbed by young Wilf Courtney. Of course there had been no proof, no tangible evidence but she had found her back door open and had seen Wilf scrambling over her wall. When she returned to the kitchen her crocodile handbag complete with pension had vanished.

Joan Gravely, a widow, was a kind soul, who had given much of her own time to champion good causes and she didn't deserve to be rooked in this way. How many down and outs had she helped? How many homeless people had she taken in? Her good Christian spirit was well known; Saint Joan some people called her.

Karl decided that it was about time young Wilf was tackled and he was just the person to do it.

The clocks had gone back. It would be dark by half past five, dark enough to cloak his activities. He cashed up, left the shop, dropping the day's takings at the bank. He had a chat with Janice, one of the tellers at the bank. He always thought her job title suited her for that was exactly what she was, a teller of news.

In fact most of his tips about injustice had come from her.

The gossip at the counter was news of the underwear thief who had been pinching women's undies from washing lines in the area. He had spread his net further and had bigger things on his mind. Mrs. Montmorency, an unusually large woman, with a personality to match, had found her pink bloomers, and bra, which in Janice's terms was big enough to hold two churns, and her naughty nightie, the only one, she protested that she possessed, had been taken from her line. Then, to add insult to injury the line had come down muddying the rest of her washing so it all had to be put through its wash cycle again. The thought of anyone, as it were, 'getting off' on Mrs. M's undies was a source of huge amusement. All agreed he must be some sort of pervert.

More tittle-tattle followed. The vagrant, who had arrived in the town eight months ago had moved on. He had been taken in by Saint Joan who had tried to help him with his problems and alcoholism. John Knight had moved on regaining sufficient- confidence to return to his family. This was excellent news. John Knight was an intelligent old man, clearly well educated, good chess player too, by all accounts, who through life's misfortunes had become dependent on the solace provided by a bottle of booze.

Karl popped into Betsy's Cafe for his Wednesday cup of coffee and roll where he heard about a dispute between old man Partridge and his neighbour, Walter Keen, over the height of the border hedge. Karl promised himself he'd take a look.

He made his way to Whistler's End and could see exactly what was upsetting Mr. Partridge, who had lived in the town all his life. The newcomer had allowed the hedge, which adjoined their properties to grow out of control blocking out most of the daylight from Mr. Partridge's front room but Mr. Keen enjoyed privacy with no such inconvenience as theft of light. The matter was made worse because Mr. Partridge relied on his painting to keep him busy and happy. With the reduction in light that little bit of pleasure was being denied him. Karl wondered what he could do as he walked on to the sanctuary of his garage.

The racing green Peugeot 406 sat there. It would be a while before he had the courage to drive again. He turned the engine over and tinkered under the bonnet, cleaning the spark plugs, checking connections, until day had passed to twilight and twilight to the gentle comfort of the dark.

Karl slammed the hood of the car. He walked to his locker, which housed his gear. He changed his bloodied blue and white striped apron, tossed his straw boater with its characteristic, matching hatband and donned the anonymous, serviceable black slacks and polo shirt, balaclava and ski mask of the cat burglar.

Wilf Courtney lived three doors down. The alley which linked the back to back houses, usually empty, except late at night when amorous courting couples and the odd stray tom cat out on the prowl frequented it, would provide entry to Wilf's garden and access to his house and belongings, maybe even Mrs. Gravely's bag. Karl began to feel assured. That telltale prickle of excitement, which he'd missed so much sparkled down his spine. A cheery whistle of a favourite tune escaped his lips. He smiled. It was a broad smile.

He felt good and it was time!

He popped his head out of the door and scanned the alley. There was no one around. He slipped out of the door, adopting the sidelong crab-like walk of his all time hero, Bruce Lee. He scuttled along turning his head this way and that making sure there was no one to see and no one to hear. Moments later he was in the garden. He squatted beside the compost heap of lawn clippings and scanned the back of the house. He couldn't see any lights. What was the time?

Wilf worked an afternoon and early evening shift at the chipboard factory fifteen miles away. He wouldn't be back until nine or ten that night; plenty of time to do what he had to do. Wilf's mother was a barmaid at the Lazy Landlord pub working every night from six. There was no Mr. Courtney. 'The Domino', was what Karl liked to call himself. He'd read somewhere that in America it meant a cover or partial cover of the face, and after each deed he would strategically place a tile from a set of dominoes.

Karl spider scurried down the garden to the back door. He was alert now feeling fighting fit. He unrolled the black leather wallet holding his picks, metal rods and flat keys and selected the tool for the job. The pencil beam light from his torch was dim. The battery needed changing. It wasn't easy. He understood how Mel Brooks must have felt as the cross-eyed governor in 'Blazing Saddles'. When he couldn't get the pen in the holder he was told to think of his secretary, and it did the trick. Karl couldn't think of Nesta as she was now but he tried to remember her, as she was when they met. Bingo! The pick clicked the lock and the door opened. Karl crept inside closing the door softly behind him. All was still, but he needed more light. He rummaged under the sink and found a flashlight.

The kitchen was a mess. Mrs. Courtney clearly had no love of housework. The sink was piled high with food-encrusted dishes. A droning blue bottle buzzed lazily around the debris. It reminded him of an old-fashioned war plane, a bomber. It was joined by another and together they blitzkrieged the rotting waste food on the plates. The petrol blue of their fat dive-bomber bodies glinted in the light. It was not going to be easy to find anything in this chaos.

He moved swiftly through the kitchen, into the hall and picked his way up the stairs loaded on either side with towers of newspapers and magazines. Didn't the woman throw anything away? He kicked at the door at the top of the landing, which revealed an offensive disorderly sight of sopping wet towels and dirty clothing. Karl took a few more steps across the landing to the next room. This obviously belonged to Mrs. Courtney. The double bed was covered in feminine garments. The top drawer in the dressing table was open and filled up with an assortment of makeup items. Shoes littered the floor. What was this thing women had for shoes? Nesta was the same. She must have about forty pairs. He had four and as he had said he couldn't wear them all at once so what was the point?

The next room was filled with boxes and cases. Karl surmised it was all storage so the adjoining room had to be Wilf's. Karl opened the door and was impressed by its neatness. Everything was put away in regulation, no, military order. Even the drawers were labelled, work pants, best pants, work socks, best socks etc. Karl opened the wardrobe door and began to rummage through the shelves and boxes in view. He came to one marked 'Miscellaneous'. Inside was a jumble of women's underwear and on top were Mrs. Montmerency's large horse gum pink knickers together with her outsize bra and naughty nightie. Karl laughed. So, young Wilf was the underwear thief. He could utilise that information and utilise it well.

Karl probed further. There was Mrs. Gravely's distinctive crocodile handbag. Her wallet was there but empty of money. He delved further into the roomy bag and pulled out a fistful of pension and benefit books.

"What the..?" His voice was loud in the darkened room and he made himself jump.

He rifled through them, peering at the names; John Knight, he was the guy who had just moved on. Why would he leave his pension book behind? Karl checked the stubs. They had all been cashed up to date; the next one belonged to Rosa Martin. Rosa! Of course, she had left town two years previously. Mrs. Gravely had taken her in, helped her to get back on her feet until her daughter from Irby in the Wirral had contacted Rosa to ask her to come and live with her family. Karl checked the date of the last cashed item. It was last week on Friday. All of the books in his possession had been cashed in the main post office in Belvedere a neighbouring town, not in Cranley. He looked at the next book; Thomas Mann. .... He couldn't recall but had a feeling he had been in town approximately five years ago. Again the book was cashed up to date. Karl was confused. Why would Mrs. Gravely still be cashing the benefits for these people?

Karl gathered the assortment of women's under clothes and laid them carefully out on Wilf's bed and left a note on top of them.

"Return these items or I will be forced to reveal you as the pervert, underwear thief and you will be forced to suffer all the humiliation that will bring. No more nicking knickers or anything else. Keep your pilfering hands to yourself. Signed - The Domino." And he tossed a double two spotted playing piece alongside. Karl left, and retreated to his sanctuary carrying with him the tell tale crocodile bag hidden in an empty Sainsbury's bag.

Karl went to the back of the garage, took out a knapsack sprayer and filled it with a deadly mix of 'Round Up'. Not deadly to us, you understand, but deadly to all living plant life. He pulled his old butcher's bike from the back of the garage, lined it with old newspaper, put the crocodile bag at the bottom then covered it with the sprayer. Next he removed his Domino attire, donned his butcher clothes and closed his garage door. Whistling cheerfully he peddled back home.

Nesta looked hot and flustered as if hiding some secret. She plonked his dinner on the table without a word. Karl needed to talk.

"Nesta." She leapt suddenly in surprise at hearing her name. "I need your help." He hadn't spoken to her at teatime for years unless it was about the shop or routinely mundane things.

"Yes?" she queried. She hoped he didn't know what she was up to. Nesta was determined to lose weight, get fit and get some love into her life. Although she continued to wear oversize garments she was actually doing quite well and had already lost a stone in weight. Just two more to go and her size twelve figure would be back. She had just returned from her aerobics class hence the reason for her florid complexion. "What do you want? You don't ever want my help. Not on anything important."

"Well, you're wrong. I do. What can you tell me about Mrs. Gravely?"

"Kind old biddy. Why?"

"Have you heard anything about the people she's helped?"

Nesta thought this highly unusual but began to recount what Karl already knew. He noticed she was having difficulty looking at him. The trouble was she didn't know which eye to look at, his good one or the glass one. She could hardly look from eye to eye as it made her feel uncomfortable so she put her head to one side and addressed his left ear.

Karl stared at her, her face although flushed looked leaner, he interrupted her, "Have you lost weight?

"What? Oh, just a bit. I'm working on it."

"Well, good for you. Keep it up. It suits you."

Nesta blushed with pleasure. It was a long time since Karl had paid her a compliment, any compliment, and to her confusion she enjoyed it. He had said something pleasant and she didn't know how to deal with it. Nesta found herself remembering, remembering times gone by and how much they had once meant to each other and it hurt... well just a little. She recalled how much they used to laugh together. That was it! They laughed; sometimes at nothing, nothing at all. When did that all change? When did he stop admiring her bum? The last time she'd leaned over at the fridge he'd criticised, "Christ! Is that all yours?" She'd worn her jumpers and tea shirts bigger and baggier to hide the lumps and bumps she was trying so hard to iron out. He'd told her to cover up as her thighs looked like a bag of Coalite and now...now...

"Nesta, you're not listening..."

"Sorry, what did you say?"

"It doesn't matter. Just thought you could help, that's all. But it's not going to work is it?" Karl tossed down his knife and fork and walked out of the room. And so did Nesta. Karl didn't know it but he had touched Nesta. Touched her as he used to, all those years ago, when things were terrific between them. She followed him out of the room.

"Don't go!" Karl stopped and looked back. She continued, "Sorry, I meant to listen but I was caught so unawares by... by..."

"By me speaking to you, to you not just mundane stuff."

"Yes..."

Karl looked at her again. There was still that impish glint in her eye. She was still a striking woman if she had her hair done, used some makeup. Karl thrust his hand in his pocket and took out some money.

"I've got to pop out. Why don't you treat yourself tomorrow? Get a new hairstyle or something. May help you to continue with the new body image. ... It does suit you, you know." And he thrust a fifty-pound note into her hand before disappearing out of the house.

Nesta didn't know what to say. Here she was planning on getting herself looking great for some young stud she had seen down the gym and now she wasn't sure she wanted that and wondered if there wasn't something she might do to save her own marriage. It had been good, no... very good, once. Nesta went upstairs.

She ran herself a relaxing bath and stepped on the scales while the aroma of ylang ylang and sandalwood excited her senses; yes, another four pounds. She studied herself in the mirror lifting her arms above her head to see what she'd look like a stone lighter and she liked what she saw. If she could just keep it up. Nesta stepped into the bath and began her ritual of body brushing. She applied a cooling cucumber mask to her face and allowed herself to float away with past memories and joys that had once been hers.

Karl cycled towards Walter Keen's house. Damn it! The place was floodlit. How could Karl possibly do what he had to do, in full view?

Karl slunk across to the garage, found the fuse box and tripped the switch. The lights like Blackpool illuminations blinked into velvet darkness. He waited quietly. Fortunately there was no roar from inside. No one came rushing out. Walter must be away. Good! That would give him time to do the deed. Karl strapped on the sprayer and proceeded to spray all he could of the hedge and root system. He strewed a few dominoes on the soft earth under the foliage, returned to the garage and tripped the switch again. The lights blazed once more and Karl made his escape.

When he returned the house was in subdued lighting. Nesta was at the top of the stairs. A CD was playing softly. Karl recognised it as one of 'their' songs. He glanced at Nesta then stopped and stared, really stared even with his one eye he could see a change.

Nesta had removed her hairpins holding the severe scraped off the face style and waves fell softly and carelessly around her face; a face glowing with a subtle application of makeup. Her eyes instead of looking like black currants were smoky grey, her lashes sooty and long, and her lips, she'd always had good lips, were full, pink, glossy and parted with that gentle promise of what could be. Karl went out of the house and came in again. He couldn't believe what he was seeing. Nesta was dressed in some sort of silk leopard print nightwear, which titillated just enough and he could clearly see that she had indeed lost weight, possibly as much as a stone and a half. Karl walked up the stairs slowly savouring her perfume, which he recognised as his favourite, Pleasures, and like a little boy Nesta led him to their room.

Afterwards they lay together quietly. It was a tender, serene quiet, neither quite certain how it had all happened. Nesta felt shy almost like the first time such had been the joy of their union.

Karl was bewildered to say the least. They hadn't made love for over three years; he hadn't wanted to, but now, now he didn't know what was happening to him.

The room was tranquil yet filled with all the unspoken thoughts and feelings of two who had believed they had nothing in common, nothing to bring them together and were living in a loveless marriage. But the truth was they each had their memories, memories of how things used to be, and neither of them had ever forgotten, not really.

Nesta broke the silence, "We have to talk."

Breakfast was an experience. They sat at the table together, trying hard to build on the previous night. They knew it would take time and hard work. Karl opened the shop, a wide grin on his face. Nesta served at his side for most of the morning. Customers were used to seeing Nesta in the shop but not to witnessing such jovial exchanges between them. As they worked Nesta considered the secret Karl had shared. He was The Domino! She felt those moth wings of delight fluttering in her stomach. And Nesta prayed that in the future it would be The Dominoes who secretly helped to right injustice in Cranley.

They could hardly wait until five o'clock. Karl turned the sign on the door. He smiled at Nesta, really smiled. Nesta looked into his eyes without flinching.

"P'raps we should return the books to Newcastle? With a letter, anonymous of course," offered Nesta.

"Yes, but we need a few more facts first."

"It was pension day yesterday."

"So?"

"Well, if she is cashing them maybe she'll apply for new books. She wouldn't have gone yesterday, it would have been manic. She may go today. I could follow her and you could snoop around."

"What about the shop?"

"Why don't you go to Mrs Gravely's. See what you can learn. I'll keep things together here. Give Bert a call. He'll help out. Then, when you're back I could do some sleuthing myself. If she leaves I can follow, pretend I'm going to the gym."

"That makes sense. Ring Bert. I'll get across to Saint Joan's."

Nesta phoned the retired butcher, Bert who was more than pleased for a day's work. Karl set off for Willow Bend, a guesthouse on the corner of the main Cranley to Belvedere road.

He wheeled his bike through the open gate, up the path and rang the bell. An elderly gentleman with a walking cane answered. Karl recognised him as one of the regular boarders who'd been there a couple of years, a good chess player he'd heard someone say.

"Yes?"

"Who is it Fred?" Karl recognised Mrs. Gravely's voice. "Oh, Mr. Simons, it's you. How can I help?" She said as she joined Fred at the door.

"Nesta and I were talking and we thought it was terrible for you to lose your pension like that and we wondered if we could help in any way. We don't want to offend but wondered if you'd let us put a box in the shop for donations like. Lots of people are grateful to you who'd love to give something. What do you say?"

"I don't know... That's very kind ..."

"Then say yes."

"Why, thank you, Mr. Simons. I will." She said graciously.

Karl stared at the old lady with her soft silver hair neatly pinned in a dignified bun, her tall, straight bearing and kindly face and thought, this can't be right. There had to be some simple explanation.

"I expect you miss old Mr. Knight now he's gone, played chess with him didn't you?"

"That I did. He was a nice man," Fred said.

"We were lucky with him weren't we, Fred? Got him back on the straight and narrow. Gone back to Scotland he has, God bless him."

"Yes," affirmed Fred, gone to live with his daughter, I

understand. Happened all of a sudden it did."

"Come now, Fred, Mr Simons is a busy man and I've left the saucepan on the boil. Thank you, Mr Simons. Very kind of you. I'll call in the shop in a couple of weeks."

"Right," he knew he was being dismissed and gave a cheery wave as the front door closed. He walked slowly back down the path with his bike, his head buzzing like a computer. She seemed to be the sweet old lady everyone said she was. But before closing the door he'd noticed a steeliness about her. Her mouth had snapped shut like a rattrap on the goodbye. Was it something or just his imagination? Karl had difficulty shutting the gate, couldn't quite get the catch lined up. Damn this one eye! He eventually managed it and mounted his bike when he was stopped by a voice.

"Hsst! Over here! Walk down the block towards the shops. That's it!"

Karl recognised Fred's voice and steered his bike along the pavement. Fred appeared from behind Willow's Bend and accompanied him towards the parade of shops. He spoke urgently. "Glad you came, didn't know what to do really. I'm terrified I'll be next."

"Why? What's going on?"

"John Knight. She says he's gone back to Scotland, but if that's the case then why're his things still in his room? There's comings and goings in this house that don't add up. People come, stop a while, then vanish. Always folks no one would give a hoot about."

"Maybe they just upped and left, people do you know. P'raps Mr. Knight is having his things sent on."

"That's what she'd have you believe. His togs'll end up in a charity shop and other more personal effects burnt in the garden."

"You're making it sound like she's done him in. You're all right. You've been here some time."

"Because I get regular visits from the district nurse for my feet. Can't get rid of me at the moment." He waggled his cane at Karl. "If John Knight had moved on wouldn't he have taken his wallet with him?"

Karl had to agree that was odd but it was the next thing Fred said, which really worried him. "And then there's the smell?"

"Smell?"

"Horrible it is, from the cellar. She's always doing things down there, cementing and blocking!"

"What sort of smell?"

"Don't know how to describe it really, never smelt it before I came here. Sweet… that putrefying sweetness you get when a mouse has died somewhere and you can't track it down. Fetid like you read in books. It's the smell of death. What you going to do Mr. Simons?"

Karl wasn't quite sure what he was going to do. "How can I get in and see?"

"She'll be off to Belvedere this afternoon, always does Mondays and Fridays."

"Not on a Thursday?"

"Pension day? No. It's always too busy for her. She'll be gone later after two. I can let you in then. Come and see for yourself."

Back at the shop Bert was delighted to work for the day. Nesta announced she had a dentist appointment in Belvedere and would be a while. Karl added that he too had to pop out just for an hour.

"That's fine. I'll only be an hour on my own. I can manage." Bert replied chirpily.

Karl and Nesta grabbed a few minutes together. He recounted what had happened. They agreed Nesta would follow Saint Joan to Belvedere.

Karl returned to see Fred who showed Karl into the house. Karl examined John Knight's room. It certainly didn't look as if he'd gone away.

"Where's this cellar you're talking about?"

"This way. Follow me." Fred unlocked the door to the cellar and switched on the light, but he wouldn't follow Karl down the rickety wooden steps.

The stench of rotting flesh ambushed Karl and he fought to keep his lunch in his stomach. The dirt floor had been cemented in places and there was evidence of a newly erected brick wall. He moved to where there appeared to be some fresh digging and scraped at the soil with a spade. The tip of a hand began to show through the earth. Karl had seen and smelt enough. He rushed up the steps and regurgitated his chicken salad into the kitchen sink.

"Sorry!" Karl wiped his mouth. He tried to flush away the debris. "Do you have anywhere you can go?" Fred shook his head. "Order a taxi, come to my shop. You can stay with us until this is sorted out. Leave everything," he ordered, "Come now!"

Karl, with his arm around Nesta , watched Saint Joan being handcuffed and led away. The venerated Mrs. Gravely was a notorious female serial killer. She would never have been discovered if it wasn't for the pilfering of Wilf Courtney and the action of The Dominoes. Nesta and Karl were a team, an excellent team. Things were once again looking good.

Our Authors

Elizabeth Revill

Elizabeth started her career as professional actress on the BBC Radio Rep and worked extensively in radio and theatre with some television and film work. She still does perform occasionally. Elizabeth writes in many genres and is a multi-optioned screenwriter and playwright.

Novels

DCI Allison Thrillers:
Killing Me Softly
Prayer for the Dying
God Only Knows
Would I Lie To You?
Windows For The Dead
Dead Eyes Opened

Historical - Llewellyn Family Saga:
Whispers on the Wind
Shadows on the Moon
Rainbows in the Clouds
Thunder in the Sun

Historical – Nathaniel Brookes Novels
Against the Tide
Turn of the Tide

Thrillers
The Electra Conspiracy Part 1
The Electra Conspiracy Part 2

Stand Alone Novels:

Sanjukta and the Box of Souls - Fantasy
The Forsaken And The Damned - Historical
Web of Fear - Thriller
The Dreamtime of the Artful Dodger with Norman Eshley - Historical
The Secret of Gidon – a children's illustrated book.

More information can be found at:
www.elizabethrevill.com
www.facebook.com/profile.php?id=100063371760218

Contact: elizabethrevill@protonmail.com

Ben Fielder

After Drama School and working as an actor, in theatre and television, appearing in Down to Earth and more, Ben decided to write.

His first novel for young adults is 'Land of the Awoken' and was very well received. He has a number of other projects on the go, is an optioned screenwriter and an artist. His artwork can be found on his Facebook Page: Adrift Art Studio. His work can be found on Etsy at AdriftArtStudioBDF

He took the lead in a radio play, "Things to do in Devon when you're dead." This will soon be available on Audible.

Find Land of the Awoken here:
www.amazon.co.uk/dp/B006O2872Q

Joe Talon

Joe Talon is an author used to walking on the wild and darker side of life. A place where you're never quite certain if the world is full of rainbows or shadows.

Having grown up on Exmoor, Joe has been fascinated by the mysterious and spooky places that dwell in the dark woodlands and quiet combes. Joe has created a world just a little sideways from ours in this new series. It is full of shapes moving on the edge of our vision when they shouldn't and cold spots in warm places. For Joe, there is always the question, 'what would I do if?

> The creaking door isn't just a draught.
> The footfalls not friends but foes.
> The scream is not a crying fox, it is...

What spare time Joe has is spent with six dogs, lots of walks and exploring the strange worlds just the other side what we think we know to be real.

You can find Joe via:
joe@joetalon.com
www.joetalon.com
or on Book Bub or on Amazon and of course Facebook!

Helen Hollick

First accepted for traditional publication in 1993, Helen became a USA Today Bestseller with her historical novel, The Forever Queen (titled A Hollow Crown in the UK) with the sequel, Harold The King (US: I Am The Chosen King) being novels that explore the events that led to the Battle of Hastings in 1066. Her Pendragon's Banner Trilogy is a fifth-century version of the Arthurian legend, and she writes a nautical adventure/fantasy series, The Sea Witch Voyages. She is now also branching out into the quick read novella, 'Cosy Mystery' genre with her Jan Christopher Murder Mysteries, set in the 1970s, with the first in the series, A Mirror Murder incorporating her, often hilarious, memories of working as a library assistant. Her non-fiction books are Pirates: Truth and Tales and Life of a Smuggler.

She moved with her family from London in January 2013, and now lives in an eighteenth-century farmhouse in North Devon, not far from South Molton. She reviews some fiction, runs several blogs and occasionally gets time to write...

www.helenhollick.net
Amazon Universal Link: https://viewauthor.at/HelenHollick
Newsletter: https://tinyletter.com/HelenHollick
Blog:https://ofhistoryandkings.blogspot.com/

Bruce Aiken

Bruce, to date, has five novels published, one humorous book (many years ago), and is working on a 'cosey crime' sixth novel. All his novels are all hidden in the depths of Amazon – the retailer, not the rainforest, although both are equally easy to get lost in.

Novels
The Curious Talent of Lily Ash
Hope Island
Life After Alison
The Act of Falling
White Lies
How to do Sex Properly

Bruce Aiken has lived on Exmoor for over 50 years and, as well as writing novels, works as a freelance designer, illustrator and writer. He has worked for over 20 publishers and has won a number of awards - all of which he regards with suspicion.

www.bruceaiken.co.uk

Ian Riddle

Ian has so far published three volumes of short stories and two novels: all Published by Michael Terence Publishing.

Collected Writings Vol 1, Vol 2 & Vol 3 (2018, 2019 & 2020)

Midsummer Dreams (Published 2020)
A lyrical history of the lives, loves and, in particular, the dreams of several of the inhabitants of the small village of Treddoch Harbour. Treddoch, as it's referred to locally, is a fictional, atypical, once fishing, now touristy, community situated on Cornwall's southern coast.
YouTube:
www.youtu.be/lmrVc-hbTm8

Bewitched, Bothered, Bewildered (Published 2022)
The tale of a young writer in search of inspiration for subject matter for a second novel. On a visit to Singapore and Raffles Hotel he's helped by three writers, Miller, Maugham and Kipling all of whom have been dead for quite some time! Do they exist or is he going quietly insane?

Ian's hoping to publish what he refers to as a quasi-novel, Our Rose, My Reg, and Me later this year.
Our Rose is a set of ten short stories/monologues of equal length told across a twelve-month period. They can be read or performed individually although, when read in total and in sequence, they form something of a novel.

Legend: The Tale of Tommy Tattle, a novella set amongst the dead of a Cornish cemetery, is scheduled to be published shortly after.

For more information please visit:
www.ianriddle.co.uk

Glenda Bartlett

A mistress of comedy as can be seen in her novels set in a village in North Devon, St. Urith with Well featuring Celia Ladygarden.

She is also a part of a satirical group called The Eight Fannys and has a show called Fannying Around where the proceeds went to help the people of Ukraine.

Novels:

The Curious Curiosity
Celia Finds an Angel
The Unfurled Moth
Wedding Fever

Sarah Luddington

For broken heroes and their dangerous adventures check out my other books.

Shadow Ops:
Fortune's Soldier
Fortune's Soldier Prequel (free short story)
Ultimate Sanction
Final Play
Lancing's Journey (free short novella)
Shadow Ops Box Set

The Knights of Camelot Series:
Lancelot and the King
Lancelot and the Sword
Lancelot and the Grail
Lancelot's Challenge
Lancelot's Burden
Lancelot's Curse
Betrayal of Lancelot
Passion of Lancelot
Revenge of Lancelot
Lancelot and the Spear
Camelot's Love (free novella and prequel to the series)

Sons of Camelot Series:
Pendragon Legacy

Du Lac Legacy
Albion's Legacy
Rogue's Tale
Men of Sherwood Vol 1
Men of Sherwood Vol 2

All the following are M/M stand alone
Ares' Story
Arawn's Story
Seelie
Chords for the Dead
Queer Collection (free stories, long and short)

Michael Forester

Books in print:

Non Fiction
If It Wasn't For That Dog - the story of my first year with my hearing dog, Matt
One Journey An inspirational travelogue
Forest Rain - A collection of inspirational essays, metaphorical fiction and verse
Forest Dawn - A second collection to follow Forest Rain
Forest Pathways - A third collection, published in March 2023

Fiction
Dragonsong - An arthurian fantasy about Rebekan, daughter of Merlin
The Goblin Child - A short story collection
A Home For Other Gods - Dystopian
Vicious - An urban fantasy based on the apparent reincarnation of a 1970s punk rock star
Too - A sequel to Vicious

www.michaelforester.co.uk

David Luddington

Read On…

Terry's Story continues in the comedy novel Forever England. Available from all good bookshops and online stores in paperback, eBook or Audiobook.

Michael's Story continues in the comedy novel Camp Scoundrel. Available from all good bookshops and online stores in paperback, eBook or Audiobook.

John's Story continues in the comedy novel Whose Reality is this Anyway. Available from all good bookshops and online stores in paperback, eBook or Audiobook.

Tony's Story begins in the comedy novel The Return of The Hippy. Available from all good bookshops and online stores in paperback, eBook or Audiobook.

I also have: The Money That Never Was, Schrodinger's Cottage, The Bank of Goodliness, The Rose Well Files, King of Scanlon's Rock

If you are interest in finding out more about my writing then please visit my website where you can join my friends list. From time to time I can then randomly send you updates, comedy snippets or news. luddington.com/newsletter/

Helen Garlick

Author of:
No Place to Lie, published by Whitefox shorturl.at/iwzLV

www.helengarlick.com
YouTube: Hello! It's Better to Talk shorturl.at/qDQ35

Mark Blackburn

Mark has recently been announced by Dame Margaret Drabble

as the Runner-Up in the Interact Ruth Rendell Short Story Prize. She personally selected his work, saying how much she loved and related to it. He was also shortlisted last summer for the TLC Pen Factor Pitch Prize 2022.

After working as a shoe-seller and in property in London, he now lives in Somerset, England, doing what he loves best - writing. His main work-in-progress is this full-length work of creative non-fiction, *Final Approach: My Book of Airports*. Extracts have won him a trip to Sydney and have been published or shortlisted by Moxy literary magazine, the A3 Review, Fish Publishing and others. He has written a number of short stories and other pieces of creative non-fiction which have been published online and in print.

He's also written a book for local children confined to home during lockdown. This has now been published more widely to a great reception. A sequel will be out this summer.

He regularly reads and performs his work in the UK, and appears in the media talking about his writing and the writing process. He has a considerable social media presence with over 6,000 followers across Facebook, Twitter and Instagram.

markblackburn.co.uk
facebook.com/MarkBlackburn/Writer
twitter.com/markblackburn
instagram.com/mdhblackburn

Tim Prescott

Tim has had a varied career. He has written film shorts and screenplays as well as plays for the stage and radio. He is also a performer and expert in Tai Chi.

His most notable work includes:

Beach Impediment Festival Fringe Comedy
Things to Do in Devon When you're Dead Audio Drama 2023
The Knockout Screenplay
The one man show, "The Boxer."

N. Joy

Other works:

Jill
Murderlicious
Wands up Witches
The Witches of Amerlie

Tom Barfett

Tom, an Oxford graduate, served in the Church of England in Gosport, London, Penzance, Falmouth and Hereford. He was a member of both the diocesan and national Synods and was also a Church Commissioner. He was a chaplain in the Order of St. John and was also granted the honour of being appointed a Queen's Chaplain.

He wrote many sermons and the occasional short story, including this one written in 1945.

Lucienne Boyce

Lucienne Boyce writes historical fiction, nonfiction and biography. Her historical novels to date are To The Fair Land, an eighteenth-century thriller; and the Dan Foster Mysteries (Bloodie Bones, The Butcher's Block, Death Makes No Distinction, and The Contraband Killings. The Fatal Coin is a prequel Dan Foster Mystery novella.) Her non-fiction books are The Bristol Suffragettes and The Road to Representation: Essays on the Women's Suffrage Campaign; as well as contributions to other books.

Books by Lucienne Boyce

Dan Foster Mysteries
Bloodie Bones
The Butcher's Block
Death makes no Distinction
The Contraband Killings
The Fatal Coin
Stand alone
To the Fairland
The Bristol Suffragettes

Discover all her work at:
www.lucienneboyce.com

Colin Leamon

A Teddy Bear's Tale
Rebecca the Unicorn

Other short stories can be found on Amazon Kindle.
www.stoll.org.uk/no-homeless-veterans/

Elizabeth St.John

Elizabeth's critically acclaimed historical fiction novels tell the stories of her ancestors: extraordinary women whose intriguing kinship with England's kings and queens brings an intimately unique perspective to Medieval, Tudor, and Stuart times.

Inspired by family archives and residences from Lydiard Park to Nottingham Castle and the Tower of London, Elizabeth spends much of her time exploring ancestral portraits, diaries, and lost gardens. And encountering the occasional ghost. But that's another story.

Elizabeth's books include her trilogy, The Lydiard Chronicles, set in 17th Century England during the Civil War, and her newest release, The Godmother's Secret, which explores the medieval mystery of the missing Princes in the Tower of London.

website: http://www.elizabethjstjohn.com/

Richard Williams

I am a retired local government lawyer filling my time with charity work and trying to write a novel. The first draft is complete but in need of a significant edit! I am a trustee of Emmaus Cornwall so this project is very close to my heart. We have established a growing tree nursery (pardon the pun) and are looking to establish a Community as soon as we can! To relax, I write quizzes, act in a Murder, Mystery troupe and fanatically support a very under-achieving football team!

And Finally

Blue Poppy Publishing is a small but rapidly growing publisher based in Devon. As such, it does not have a multi-million pound budget to promote books such as this. In fact, there are times when there is not even a *multi-pound* budget. As such, we implore you, if you have enjoyed this book even a little, to tell others about it. Write a review, post about it on social media, or talk to people in person. Every penny of profit from sales of this book goes to support the vital work that Emmaus does.

Yes, you can also lend it to people; not everyone has money to spend on books, but they should still be able to read it, and they might then tell someone else who will buy it.

As has already been said, every professional involved in the production of this book has given their time free of charge, so I trust it is not too much to ask you for some free public relations and advertising from you.

Visit www.bluepoppypublishing.co.uk to find out more.